Tourmalin's Time Cheques by F. Anstey

F. Anstey was the pseudonym of Thomas Anstey Guthrie who was born in Kensington, London on August 8th, 1856, to Augusta Amherst Austen, an organist and composer, and Thomas Anstey Guthrie., a prosperous military tailor

Anstey was educated at King's College School and then at Trinity Hall, Cambridge. Although his education was first rate Anstey could only manage a third-class degree; A Gentlemen's degree as it was euphemistically known.

In 1880 he was called to the bar. However this career path rapidly fell away in his desire to become an author. The successful publication of Vice Versa, in 1882, with the premise of a substitution of a father for his schoolboy son, made his name and reputation as a refreshing and original humorist.

The following year he published a rather more serious work, The Giant's Robe. Interestingly the story is about a plagiarist and Anstey was, ironically, accused of plagiarism in writing the work. Despite good reviews both he and his public knew that his writing career was to be that of a humorist.

In the following years he published prolifically beginning with; The Black Poodle (1884), The Tinted Venus (1885), A Fallen Idol (1886), and Baboo Jabberjee B.A. (1897).

Anstey worked not only as a novelist and short story writer but was also a valued member of the staff at the humorous Punch magazine, in which his voces populi and his parodies of a reciter's stock-piece (Burglar Bill) represent perhaps his best work.

In 1901, his successful farce, The Man from Blankleys, based on a story that originally appeared in Punch, was first produced on stage at the Prince of Wales Theatre, in London.

Anstey had become a writer, and a successful one at that, of many talents.

Many more of his stories were made into plays and films over the years. Others were simply taken for the premise alone, usually with no credit to the original author.

By the end of the First World War Anstey's original publications had slowed to a crawl and he seemed rather more interested in translating and publishing some works of Moliere.

Thomas Anstey Guthrie died of pneumonia on March 10th, 1934 in London.

His self-deprecating autobiography, A Long Retrospect, was published in 1936.

Index of Contents

THE PROLOGUE

Mr. Peter Tourmalin was sitting, or rather lying, in a steamer-chair on the first-class saloon-deck of the P. and O. steamer Boomerang, which had not been many days as yet on the voyage home from Sydney. He had been trying to read; but it was a hot morning, and the curry, of which he had partaken freely at breakfast, had made him feel a little heavy and disinclined for mental exertion just then, particularly as Buckle's History of Civilisation, the first volume of which he had brought up from the ship's library, is not exactly light literature at any time.

He wanted distraction of some sort, but he could not summon up sufficient energy to rise and pace the deck, as his only acquaintance on board, a Mr. Perkins, was doing with a breezy vigour which Tourmalin found himself feebly resenting.

Another alternative was open to him, it is true: not far away were other deck-chairs, in which some of the lady passengers were reading, writing, and chatting more or less languidly. There were not very many on board—for it was autumn, a time at which homeward-bound vessels are not apt to be crowded;—but even in that small group there were one or two with whom it might have seemed possible to pass a little time in a pleasant and profitable manner. For instance, there was that tall, graceful girl in the navy-blue skirt, and the striped cotton blouse confined at her slender waist by a leathern belt. (Tourmalin, it should be mentioned, was in the habit of noticing the details of feminine costume.) She had regular features, grey eyes which lighted up whenever she spoke, and an expression of singular nobility and sweetness; her fair hair was fastened up in loose gleaming masses under her highly becoming straw hat.

Peter watched her surreptitiously, from time to time, from behind the third page of Buckle. She was attempting to read a novel; but her attention, like his own, wandered occasionally, and he even fancied that he surprised her now and then in the act of glancing at himself with a certain interest.

Near her was another girl, not quite so tall, and darker, but scarcely less pleasing in appearance. She wore a cool-looking pink frock, and her luxuriant bronze tresses were set off by a simple white-flannel cap. She held some embroidery in her listless fingers, but was principally occupied in gazing out to sea with a wistful and almost melancholy expression. Her eyes were soft and brown, and her features piquantly irregular; giving Peter, who considered himself no mean judge of female character, the impression of a highly emotional and enthusiastic temperament. He thought he saw signs that she also honoured him by her notice.

Peter was a flat-headed little man, with weak eyes and flaxen hair; but even flat-headed little men may indulge these fancies at times, without grossly deceiving themselves. He knew, as one does learn such things on board ship, that the name of the first young lady was Tyrrell, and that she was the daughter of a judge who had been spending the Long Vacation in a voyage to recruit his health. Of the other, he knew no more than that she was a Miss Davenport.

At present, however, he had no personal acquaintance with either of them, and, in fact, as has already been said, knew nobody on board to speak to, except the energetic Mr. Perkins, a cheery man with a large fund of general information, who was going home on some business connected with a banking house in Melbourne.

And yet it is not difficult to make acquaintances on board ship, if a man cares to do so; accident or design will provide opportunities in plenty, and two or three days at sea are equivalent to at least as many weeks on shore. And Peter being quite aware of these facts, and by no means indifferent to the society of the other sex, which, indeed, he considered more interesting than that of his own, it would seem that he must have had some strong reason for having kept studiously apart from the social life on board the Boomerang.

He had a reason, and it was this: he was an engaged man, and on his probation. A bachelor, still under thirty, of desultory habits which unfitted him to shine in any profession, he had a competency—that refuge of the incompetent—which made him independent.

Some months previously he had had the good fortune to meet with a lady somewhat his junior in years, but endowed with charms of mind and character which excited his admiration and reverence. He recognised that she supplied the qualities in which he felt himself deficient; he was weary of the rather purposeless life he had led. He wanted a wife who would regulate and organise his existence; and Miss Sophia Pinceney, with her decision and her thoroughness, was eminently the person to do it. So it was not long before he took courage and proposed to her.

Miss Pinceney, though she had been highly educated, and possessed a considerable fortune of her own, was by no means inclined to look unfavourably upon such a suitor. He might not be quite her intellectual equal, but he was anxious to improve his mind. He was amiable and amenable, and altogether likely, under careful guidance, to prove an excellent husband.

But she was prudent, and reason told her that the suddenness of Peter's passion was no guarantee of its enduring qualities. She had heard and seen too much of a rather catholic susceptibility in his nature, to feel it safe to incur so grave a risk as marriage until she had certain proof that his attachment to her was robust enough to bear the severest test; and to that test she was determined to submit him.

She consented to an engagement on one condition, that he was to take a long voyage. If he returned in the same mind, she would be sufficiently sure of his constancy to marry him as soon as he wished: if he did not, her misgivings would be amply justified. There was very little sentiment about Sophia; she took a practical and philosophical view of the marriage union, as became a disciple of Ibsen.

"I like you, Peter," she told him frankly; "you have many qualities that endear you to me, but I don't feel that I can depend upon you at present. And from what I know of you, I fear it is only too probable that absence and the attractive society of a passenger-ship may lead you to discover that you have mistaken the depth of the feeling you entertain for me."

"But, look here, Sophia," he had expostulated; "if you're afraid of that, why do you make me go?"

"Because," she had replied, with her admirable common-sense, "because, if my fears should prove to be unhappily only too well-founded, I shall, at least, have made the discovery before it is too late."

And, in spite of all his protests, Peter had to go. Sophia sought to reconcile him to this necessity by pointing out the advantages of travel, the enlarging effect it would have upon his mind, and the opportunities a long sea-voyage afforded for regular and uninterrupted study on the lines she had already mapped out for him; but, despite these consolations, he went away in low spirits. When the moment came for parting, even the strong-minded Sophia was seized with a kind of compunction.

"Something tells me, Peter," she said, "that the ordeal will prove too much for you: in spite of your good resolutions, you will sooner or later be drawn into some flirtation which will make you forget me. I know you so well, Peter!"

"I wish you could show a little more confidence in me," he had answered, in a wounded tone. "Since I met you, Sophia, I have ceased to be the butterfly I was. But as you seem to doubt me, it may relieve your mind if I promise faithfully that, while I am away from you, I will never, under any inducement, allow myself to overstep the limits of the most ordinary civility towards any woman with whom I may be brought in contact. I swear it, Sophia! Are you satisfied now?"

Perhaps he had a secret prevision that a time might come when this oath would prove a salutary restraint upon his straying fancy, and it certainly had an immediate and most reassuring effect upon Sophia.

Tourmalin had gone out to Australia, had seen something of the country during his stay in the colony, and was now, as we have seen, on his return; and during the whole time his oath, to his great credit, had been literally and faithfully kept.

During the voyage out, he had been too persistently unwell to be inclined to dally with sentiment; but in his subsequent wanderings, he had avoided, or rather escaped, all intercourse with any Colonial ladies who might by any possibility affect his allegiance to Sophia, whose image consequently still held undisputed possession of his heart.

In case he should feel himself wavering at any time, he had been careful to provide himself with a talisman in the shape of a photograph, the mere sight of which would be instantly effectual. But somehow, since he had been on board the Boomerang, the occasions on which he had been driven to refer to this photograph had been growing more and more frequent; while, at the same time, he had a tormenting consciousness that it took an increasingly longer time to work.

He brought it out now, and studied it attentively. It was the likeness of a girl without any great pretensions to beauty, with dark hair rolled neatly back from a massive brow that shone with intellectuality; penetrating eyes, whose keenness was generally tempered by folding-glasses; a large, firm mouth, and a square chin: altogether, the face of a young woman who would stand no trifling.

He put it back respectfully in his pocket; but the impulse to go across and drop, in an accidental fashion, into a vacant seat near one of those two girls was still unconquered. He was feeling so dull; he had got such a very little way into the History of Civilisation, a work which he was reading rather for Sophia's satisfaction than his own, and there was such a lot more of it! Might he not allow himself a brief holiday, and beguile the long weary morning with a little cheerful conversation? It was most unlikely, strict etiquette being by general consent suspended on board ship, that either young lady would resent a hazarded remark—at all events, he could but try.

But then his oath—his rash and voluntary oath to Sophia—what of that? He had not, it was true, debarred himself from ordinary civility; but could he be sure of keeping always within those bounds if the acquaintanceship was once established? He had reasons for doubting this very seriously. And, besides, had not Sophia more than hinted in her last letter that, as a reward for his fidelity, she might join the ship at Gibraltar with her mother, and so put an earlier end to his term of probation? He could not be too careful. After holding out so long, it would be madness to relax his precautions now. No, he would resist these Sirens, like a modern Ulysses; though, in the latter's case, the Sirens were not actually on board, and, even then, the hero had to be lashed to the mast. But Tourmalin felt confident, notwithstanding, that he would prove at least as obdurate as the wily Greek.

He was not a strong-minded man; but he had one quality which is almost as valuable a safeguard against temptation as strength of mind—namely, timidity.

His love for his betrothed was chastened by a considerable dash of awe, and he was resolved not to compromise himself in her eyes just for the sake of a little temporary distraction.

At this point of his deliberations he looked at his watch: it was close upon twelve; only one hour to be got through before tiffin. Why, an hour was nothing; he could surely contrive to kill it over Buckle! A little courage, a little concentration, and he would certainly attain to an interest in "the laws which govern human actions."

The ship's bells were just striking; he counted the strokes: one, two, three, four, five—and no more! There must be some mistake; it could not possibly be only half-past ten. Why, it was hours since breakfast!

"Looking at your watch, eh?" said his friend Perkins, as he reached Peter's chair for about the hundredth time. "Ah! you're fast, I see. Haven't altered your watch yet? They've put the ship's clock back again this morning; nearly half-an-hour it was this time—it was rather less yesterday and the day before: we shall go on gaining so much extra time a day, I suppose, till we get to Gib."

"You don't mean to tell me that!" exclaimed Peter, with a half-suppressed groan. If the time had seemed tedious and interminable enough before, how much more so was it now! How infinitely greater would the effort be to fix his thoughts resolutely on Buckle, and ignore the very existence of his distracting neighbours, now that it was to be daily prolonged in this exasperating manner!

"You don't seem to appreciate the arrangement?" remarked the Manager, as he allowed himself to drop cautiously—for he was a bulky man—into a hammock-chair beside Tourmalin.

"Appreciate it!" said Peter, with strong disgust. "Aren't there enough half-hours, and confoundedly long ones, too, in the day as it is, without having extra ones forced on you like this? And giving it to us in the daytime, too! They might at least put the clock back at night, when it wouldn't so much matter. I do think it's very bad management, I must say!"

His companion began a long explanation about the meridian, and sun's time, and ship's time, and Greenwich time, to which Peter gave but a very intermittent attention, so stupefied did he feel at this unwelcome discovery.

"It's a curious thing to think of," the other was saying thoughtfully, "that a man, by simply making a voyage like this, should make a clear gain of several hours which he would never have had at all if he had stayed at home!"

"I would much rather be without them" said Peter. "I find it quite difficult enough to spend the time as it is; and how on earth I can spend any more, I don't know!"

"Why spend it, then?" asked his friend quietly.

"What else am I to do with it?"

"What else? See here, my friend; when you have an amount of spare cash that you've no immediate use for, you don't let it lie idle at home, do you? You pay it in to your credit at a bank, and let it remain on deposit till you do want it—eh? Well, then, why not treat your spare time as you would your spare cash. Do you see what I mean?"

"Not altogether," confessed Peter, considerably puzzled.

"It's simple enough nowadays. For instance, the establishment I have the honour to be connected with—the Anglo-Australian Joint Stock Time Bank Limited—confines itself, as you are doubtless aware, almost entirely to that class of business."

"Ah!" said Peter, no more enlightened than before, "does it indeed? Would you mind explaining what particular class of business it carries on? I don't quite understand."

"Bless my soul, sir!" said the Manager, rather irritably, "you must be uncommonly ignorant of financial matters not to have heard of this before! However, I will try to make it clear to you. I daresay you have heard that 'Time is Money'? Very well, all our operations are conducted on that principle. We are prepared to make advances, on good security of course, of time to almost any amount; and we are simply overwhelmed with applications for loans. Business men, as you may know, are perpetually pressed for time, and will consent to almost anything to obtain it. Our transactions in time, sir, are immense. Why, the amount of Time passing through our books annually during the last ten years, averages—ah! about sixty centuries! That's pretty well, I think, sir?"

He was so perfectly business-like and serious that Peter almost forgot to see anything preposterous in what he said.

"It sounds magnificent," he said politely; "only, you see, I don't want to borrow any time myself. I've too much on my hands already."

"Just so," said the Manager; "but if you will kindly hear me out, I am coming to that. Lending time is only one side of our business; we are also ready to accept the charge of any spare time that customers may be willing to deposit with us, and, with our experience and facilities, I need hardly say that we are able to employ it to the best advantage. Now, say, for example, that you wish to open an account with us. Well, we'll take these spare half-hours of yours that are only an encumbrance to you at present, and if you choose to allow them to remain on deposit, they will carry interest at five per cent. per month; that is, five minutes on every hour and three-quarters, roughly, for each month, until you withdraw them. In that way alone, by merely leaving your time with us for six months you will gain—now, let me see—over three additional hours in compound interest on your original capital of ten hours or so. And no previous notice required before withdrawal! Let me tell you, sir, you will not find many banks do business on such terms as that!"

"No," said Peter, who could not follow all this arithmetic, "so I should imagine. Only, I don't quite see, if you will pardon my saying so, what particular advantage I should gain if I did open an account of this sort."

"You don't? You surprise me, you really do. Here are you, with these additional hours lying idle on your hands: you didn't expect 'em, and don't want 'em. But how do you know that you mayn't be glad of 'em at some time or other? Just think how grateful you might be hereafter, if you could get back a single one of these half-hours which you find so tedious now. Half-an-hour on board a fine ship like this, splendid weather, bracing sea-air, perfect rest, pleasant company, and so on—why, you'd be willing to pay any money for it! Well, bank your extra time; and you can draw every individual hour in quarters, halves, or wholes, when you please and as you please. That's the advantage of it, sir!"

"I think I see," said Peter: "only, how am I to make the deposit in the first instance?"

"That's easily arranged. The captain can't compel you to accept the time now by merely putting back the hands of the clock, can he? So, all you have to do is to abstain from altering your watch so long as you are on board, and to fill up a little form; after which I shall be happy to supply you with a book of Time Cheques, which you can fill up and present whenever you wish to spend a given number of minutes in the pleasantest possible of ways."

"But where am I to present these cheques?" inquired Peter.

"Oh!" said the Manager, "there will be no difficulty whatever about that. Any clock will cash it for you—provided, of course, that it hasn't stopped. You merely have to slip your cheque underneath or behind it, and you will at once be paid whatever amount of time the cheque is drawn for. I can show you one of our forms if you like?"

Here he brought out a bulky leather case, from which he extracted a printed document, which he handed to Peter.

Peter, however, being naturally cautious, felt a hesitation which he scarcely liked to confess.

"You see," he said, "the fact is, I should like to know first ... I've never been engaged in a—a transaction of this kind before; and, well—what I mean is, do I incur any risk of—er—a supernatural character?... It isn't like that business of Faust's, eh, don't you know?"

The Manager took back the paper with an abruptness which showed that his temper was ruffled by this suspicion.

"My good sir!" he said, with a short offended laugh, "don't, on any account, imagine that I care two pins whether you become a depositor or not. I daresay our house will continue to exist without your account. As for liability, ours is a limited concern; and, besides, a deposit would not constitute you a shareholder. If you meant anything more—well, I have still to learn that there's anything diabolical about me, sir! I simply thought I was doing you a good turn by making the suggestion; and, besides, as a business man, I never neglect any opportunity, however small. But it's entirely as you please, I'm sure."

There was nothing in the least demoniacal, even in his annoyance, and Peter was moved to contrition and apology.

"I—I really beg your pardon!" he said. "I do hope I haven't offended you; and, if you will allow me, I shall consider it a personal favour to be allowed to open an account with your bank. It would certainty be a great convenience to draw some of this superfluous time at some future day, instead of wasting it now. Where do I sign the form?"

The Manager was appeased; and produced the form once more, indicating the place for the signature, and even providing a stylograph-pen for the purpose. It was still somewhat of a relief to Peter's mind to find that the ink it contained was of the ordinary black hue.

"And now, about cheques," said his friend, after the signature had been obtained. "How many do you think you would require? I should say that, as the deposit is rather small, you will find fifty more than sufficient? We shall debit you with fifty seconds to cover the cheque-book. And we always recommend 'bearer' cheques as, on the whole, more convenient."

Peter said he would have fifty "bearer" cheques, and was accordingly given an oblong grey-green book, which, except that it was a trifle smaller, was in nowise different, outwardly, from an ordinary cheque-book. Still, his curiosity was not completely satisfied.

"There is just one question more," he said. "When I draw this time, where will it be spent?"

"Why, naturally, on board this ship," explained the Manager. "You see that the time you will get must necessarily be the extra time to which you are entitled by virtue of your passage, and which you would have spent as it accrued if you had not chosen to deposit it with us. By the way, when you are filling up cheques, we much prefer not to be called upon to honour drafts for less than fifteen minutes; as much more as you like, but not less. Well, then, we may consider that settled. I am extremely glad to have had the opportunity of obliging you; and I think I can promise that you will have no reason to repent of having made such a use of your time. I'll wish you good-bye for the present, sir!"

The Manager resumed his hygienic tramp round the deck, leaving Peter with the cheque-book in his hand. He was no longer surprised: now that he was more familiar with the idea, it seemed a perfectly natural and matter-of-fact arrangement; he only wondered that he had never thought of so obvious a plan before. And it was an immense relief to know that he had got rid of his extra hours for the present, at all events, and that he could now postpone them to a period at which they would be a boon rather than a burden.

And very soon he put the cheque-book away, and forgot all about it. The Story.

CHAPTER I

Peter Tourmalin's probation was at an end, and, what was more, he had come through the ordeal triumphantly. How he managed this, he scarcely knew; no doubt he was aided by the consciousness that the extra hours which he felt himself most liable to mis-spend had been placed beyond his disposal. At all events, when he met Sophia again, he had been able to convince her that her doubts of his constancy, even under the most trying conditions, were entirely undeserved. Now he was receiving his recompense: his engagement to Sophia was no longer conditional, but a recognised and irrevocable fact. It is superfluous to say that he was happy. Sophia had set herself to repair the deficiencies in his education and culture; she took him to scientific lectures and classical concerts, and made him read standard authors without skipping. He felt himself daily acquiring balance and seriousness, and an accurate habit of thought, and all the other qualities which Sophia wished him to cultivate.

Still, there were moments when he felt the need of halting and recovering his wind, so to speak, in the steep and toilsome climb to her superior mental level—times when he felt that his overtaxed brain absolutely required relaxation of some sort.

He felt this particularly one dreary morning, late in November, as he sat in his London chambers, staring with lack-lustre eyes at the letter he had that day received from his betrothed. For although they met nearly every day, she never allowed one to pass without a letter—no fond and foolish effusion, be it understood, but a kind of epistolary examination-paper, to test the progress he was making. This one contained some searching questions on Buckle's History of Civilisation, which he was expected to answer by return of post. He was not supposed to look at the book, though he had; and even then he felt himself scarcely better fitted to floor the tremendous posers devised by Sophia's unwearying care.

The day before, he had had "search-questions" in English poetry from Chaucer to Mr. Lewis Morris, which had thinned and whitened his hair; but this was, if possible, even worse.

He wished now that he had got up his Buckle more thoroughly during his voyage on the Boomerang— and, with the name, his arrangement with the Manager suddenly rose to his recollection. What had he done with that book of Time Cheques? If he could only get away, if but for a quarter of an hour—away from those sombre rooms, with their outlook on dingy housetops and a murky rhubarb-coloured sky,—if he could really exchange all that for the sunniness and warmth and delicious idleness which had once seemed so tedious, what a rest it would be! And would he not return after such an interlude with all his faculties invigorated, and better able to cope with the task he now found almost insuperable?

The first thing was to find the cheque-book, which did not take him long; though when he had found it, something made him pause before filling up a cheque. What if he had been made a fool of—if the Anglo-Australian Joint Stock Time Bank Limited never existed, or had suspended payment? But that was easily settled by presenting a cheque. Why should he not, just by way of experiment? His balance was intact as yet; he was never likely to need a little ready time more than he did just then. He would draw the minimum amount, fifteen minutes, and see how the system worked.

So, although he had little real confidence that anything would happen at all, he drew a cheque, and slipped it behind the frivolous and rather incorrect little ormolu clock upon his chimneypiece.

The result was instantaneous, and altogether beyond his expectations! The four walls of his room assumed the transparency of gauze for a second, before fading entirely away; the olive fog changed to translucent blue; there was a briny breath in the air, and he himself was leaning upon the rail at the forward end of the hurricane-deck of the Boomerang, which was riding with a slow and stately rise and fall over the heaving swell.

That was surprising enough; but more surprising still was the discovery that he was apparently engaged in close and confidential conversation with a lovely person in whom he distinctly recognised Miss Tyrrell.

"Yes, I forgive you, Mr. Tourmalin," she was saying, with an evident effort to suppress a certain agitation; "but indeed, indeed, you must never speak to me like that again!"

Now, as Peter was certainly not conscious of ever having spoken to her at all in his life, this was naturally a startling and even embarrassing beginning.

But he had presence of mind enough to take in the position of affairs, and adapt himself to them. This was one of the quarters of an hour he would have had, and it was clear that in some portion or other of his spare time he would have made Miss Tyrrell's acquaintance in some way. Of course, he ought to have been paid that particular time first; but he could easily see from her manner, and the almost tender friendliness which shone in her moistened eyes, that at this period they had advanced considerably beyond mere acquaintanceship. There had been some little mistake probably; the cheques had been wrongly numbered perhaps, or else they were honoured without regard to chronological sequence, which was most confusing.

Still, he had nothing to do but conceal his ignorance as well as he could, and pick up the loose threads as he went along. He was able, at all events, to assure her that he would not, if he could help it, incur her displeasure by speaking to her "like that" in future.

"Thanks," she said. "I know it was only a temporary forgetfulness; and—and if what you suspect should prove to be really true—why, then, Mr. Tourmalin, then, of course, you may come and tell me so."

"I will," he said; "I shall make a point of it. Only," he thought to himself, "she will have to tell me first what I'm to tell her."

"And in the meantime," she said, "let us go on as before, as if you had never brought yourself to confide your sad story to me."

So he had told a sad story, had he? he thought, much bewildered; for, as he had no story belonging to him of that character, he was afraid he must have invented one, while, of course, he could not ask for information.

"Yes," he said, with great presence of mind, "forget my unhappy story—let it never be mentioned between us again. We will go on as before—exactly as before."

"It is our only course," she agreed. "And now," she added, with a cheerfulness that struck him as a little forced, "suppose we talk of something else."

Peter considered this a good suggestion, provided it was a subject he knew a little more about; which, unhappily, it was not.

"You never answered my question," she reminded him.

He would have liked, as Ministers say in the House, "previous notice of that question;" but he could hardly say so in so many words.

"No," he said. "Forgive me if I say that it is a—a painful subject to me."

"I understand that," she said, gently (it was more than he did); "but tell me only this: was it that that made you behave as you did? You are sure you had no other reason?"

["If I say I had," thought Peter, "she will ask me what it was."] "I will be as frank as possible, Miss Tyrrell," he replied. "I had no other reason. What other reason could I have had?"

"I half fancied—but I ought to have seen from the first that, whatever it was, it was not that. And now you have made everything quite clear."

"I am glad you find it so," said Peter, with a touch of envy.

"But I might have gone on misunderstanding and misjudging, putting you down as proud and cold and unsociable, or prejudiced, but for the accident which brought us together, in spite of your determination that we should remain total strangers!"

It was an accident which had made them acquainted, then? He would draw the cheque which contained that episode of his extra time sooner or later; but it was distinctly inconvenient not to have at least some idea of what had happened.

"A fortunate accident for me, at all events!" he said, with a judicious recourse to compliment.

"It might have been a very unfortunate one for poor papa," she said, "but for you. I do believe he would have been quite inconsolable."

Peter felt an agreeable shock. Had he really been fortunate enough to distinguish himself by rescuing the Judge's fair daughter from some deadly peril? It looked very like it. He had often suspected himself of a latent heroism which had never had an opportunity of being displayed. This opportunity must have occurred, and he have proved equal to the occasion, in one of those extra hours!

"I can quite imagine that he would be inconsolable indeed!" he said gallantly. "Fortunately, I was privileged to prevent such a calamity."

"Tell me again exactly how you did it," she said. "I never quite understood."

Peter again took refuge in a discreet vagueness.

"Oh," he replied, modestly, "there's not much to tell. I saw the—er—danger, and knew there wasn't a moment to lose; and then I sprang forward, and—well, you know the rest as well as I do!"

"You only just caught him as he was going up the rigging, didn't you?" she asked.

So it was the Judge he had saved—not his daughter! Peter felt a natural disappointment. But he saw the state of the case now: a powerful judicial intellect overstrained, melancholia, suicidal impulses—it was all very sad; but, happily, he had succeeded in saving this man to his country.

"I—ventured to detain him," he said, considerately, "seeing that he was—er—rather excited."

"But weren't you afraid he would bite you?"

"No," said Peter, pained at this revelation of the Judge's condition, "that possibility did not occur to me. In fact, I am sure that—er—though the strongest intellects are occasionally subject to attacks of this sort, he would never so far forget himself as to—er—bite a complete stranger."

"Ah!" she said, "you don't know what a savage old creature he can be sometimes. He never ought to be let loose; I'm sure he's dangerous!"

"Oh! but think, Miss Tyrrell," remonstrated Peter, unmistakably shocked at this unfilial attitude towards a distinguished parent; "if he was—er—dangerous, he would not be upon the Bench now, surely!"

She glanced over her shoulder, with evident apprehension.

"How you frightened me!" she said. "I thought he was really there! But I hope they'll shut him up in future, so that he won't be able to do any more mischief. You didn't tell me how you got hold of him. Was it by his chain, or his tail?"

Peter did not know; and, besides, it was as difficult for him to picture himself in the act of seizing a hypochondriacal judge by his watch-chain or coat-tail, as it was for him to comprehend the utter want of feeling that could prompt such a question from the sufferer's own daughter.

"I hope," he said, with a gravity which he intended as a rebuke—"I hope I treated him with all the respect and consideration possible under the—er—circumstances.... I am sorry that that remark appears to amuse you!"

For Miss Tyrrell was actually laughing, with a merriment in which there was nothing forced.

"How can I help it?" she said, as soon as she could speak. "It is too funny to hear you talking of being regretful and considerate to a horrid monkey!"

"A monkey!" he repeated involuntarily.

So it was a monkey that was under restraint, and not a Judge of Her Majesty's Supreme Court of Judicature: a discovery which left him as much in the dark as to what particular service he had rendered as ever, and made him tremble to think what he might have said. But apparently, by singular good fortune, he had not committed himself beyond recovery; for Miss Tyrrell only said:

"I thought you were speaking of the monkey, the little wretch that came up behind papa and snatched away all his notes—the notes he had made for the great case he tried last term, and has to deliver judgment upon when the Courts sit again. Surely he told you how important they were, and how awkward it would have been if the monkey had escaped with them, and torn them into pieces or dropped them into the sea?—as he probably would have done, but for you!"

"Oh, ah, yes!" said Peter, feeling slightly crestfallen, for he had hoped he had performed a more dashing deed than catching a loose monkey. "I believe your father—Sir John?" he hazarded ... "Sir William, of course, thank you ... did mention the fact. But it really was such a trifling thing to do."

"Papa didn't think so," she said. "He declares he can never be grateful enough to you. And, whatever it was," she added softly, and even shyly, "I, at least, can never think lightly of a service which has—has made us what we are to one another."

What they were to one another! And what was that? A dreadful uncertainty seized upon Peter. Was it possible that, in some way he did not understand, he was engaged to this very charming girl, who was almost a stranger to him? The mere idea froze his blood; for if that was so, how did it affect his position towards Sophia? At all hazards, he must know the worst at once!

"Tell me," he said, with trembling accents,—"I know you have told me already, but tell me once more— precisely what we are to one another at present. It would be so much more satisfactory to my mind," he added, in a deprecatory tone, "to have that clearly understood."

"I thought I had made it quite clear already," she said, with the least suspicion of coldness, "that we can be nothing more to one another than friends."

The relief was almost too much for him. What a dear, good, sensible girl she was! How perfectly she appreciated the facts!

"Friends!" he cried. "Is that all? Do you really mean we are nothing more than friends?"

He caught her hand, in the fervour of his gratitude, and she allowed it to remain in his grasp; which, in the altered state of things, he found rather pleasant than otherwise.

"Ah!" she murmured, "don't ask me for more than I have said—more than I can ever say, perhaps! Let us be content with remaining friends—dear friends, if you like—but no more!"

"I will," said Peter promptly, "I will be content. Dear friends, by all means; but no more!"

"No," she assented; "unless a time should come when—"

"Yes," said Peter, encouragingly, as she hesitated. "You were about to say, a time when—?"

Her lips moved, a faint flush stole into her cheeks; she was about to complete her sentence, when her hand seemed to melt away in his own, and he stood, grasping the empty air, by his own mantelpiece. The upper deck, the heaving bows, the blue seaboard, Miss Tyrrell herself, all had vanished; and in their stead were the familiar surroundings of his chamber, the grimy London house fronts, and Sophia's list of questions lying still unanswered upon his writing-table! His fifteen minutes had come to an end; the cheque was nowhere to be seen. The minute-hand of his clock had not moved since he last saw it; but this last circumstance, as he saw on reflection, was only natural, for otherwise the Time Deposit would have conferred no real advantage, as he would never have regained the hours he had temporarily foregone.

For some time Peter sat perfectly still, with his head between his hands, occupied in a mental review of this his initial experience of the cheque-book system. It was as different as possible from the spell of perfect rest he had anticipated; but had it been unpleasant on that account? In spite of an element of mystification at starting, which was inevitable, he was obliged to admit to himself that he had enjoyed this little adventure more than perhaps he should have done. With all his attachment to Sophia, he could hardly be insensible to the privilege of suddenly finding himself the friend—and more than that, the dear friend—of so delightful a girl as this Miss Tyrrell.

There was a strange charm, a peculiar and quite platonic tenderness about an intimacy of this peculiar and unprecedented nature, which increased at every fresh recollection of it. It increased so rapidly indeed, that almost unconsciously he drew the cheque-book towards him, and began to fill up another cheque with a view to an immediate return to the Boomerang.

But when he had torn the cheque out, he hesitated. It was all quite harmless: the most severe moralist could not convict him of even the most shadowy infidelity towards his fiancée, if he chose to go back and follow up a purely retrospective episode like this—an episode which interested and fascinated him so strongly—only, what would Sophia say to it? Instinctively, he felt that the situation, innocent as it was, would fail to commend itself to her. He had no intention of informing her, it was true; but he knew that he was a poor dissembler—he might easily betray himself in some unguarded moment, and then— No! it was vexing, no doubt; but, upon the whole, it was wiser and better to renounce those additional hours on board the Boomerang altogether—to allow this past, that never had, but only might have been, to remain unsummoned and unknown for ever. Otherwise, who could tell that, by gradual assaults, even such an affection as he had for Sophia might not be eventually undermined?

But this fear, as he saw the next moment, was almost too extravagant to be seriously taken into account. He felt nothing, and never could feel anything, but warm and sincere friendship for Miss Tyrrell; and it was satisfactory to know that she was in no danger of mistaking his sentiments. Still, of course there was always a certain risk, particularly when he was necessarily in ignorance of all that had preceded and followed the only colloquy they had had as yet. At last he decided upon a compromise: he would not cash that second cheque for the present, at all events; he would reserve it for an emergency, and only use it if he was absolutely driven to do so as a mental tonic. Perhaps Sophia would not compel him to such a necessity again; he hoped—at least, he thought she would not.

So he put the unpresented cheque in an inner pocket, and set to work with desperate energy at his examination-paper; although his recent change must have proved less stimulating to his jaded faculties than he had hoped, since Sophia, after reading his answers, made the cutting remark that she scarcely knew which he had more completely failed to apprehend—the purport of his author, or that of the very simple questions she had set him.

Peter could not help thinking, rather ruefully, that Miss Tyrrell would never have been capable of such severity as that; but, then, Miss Tyrrell was not his fiancée, only a very dear friend, whom he would, most probably, never meet again.

CHAPTER II

The Second Cheque

The knowledge that one has a remedy within reach is often as effectual as the remedy itself, if not more so; which may account for the fact that, although a considerable number of weeks had elapsed since Peter Tourmalin had drawn his second cheque on the Anglo-Australian Joint Stock Time Bank Limited, that cheque still remained unpresented.

The day fixed for his wedding with Sophia was drawing near; the flat in the Marylebone Road, which was to be the scene of their joint felicity, had to be furnished, and this occupied most of his time. Sophia took the entire business upon herself, for she had scientific theories on the subject of decoration and colour harmonies which Peter could only accept with admiring awe; but, nevertheless, she required him to be constantly at hand, so that she could consult him after her own mind had been irrevocably made up.

One February afternoon he was wandering rather disconsolately about the labyrinthine passages of one of the monster upholstery establishments in the Tottenham Court Road, his chief object being to evade the courtesies of the numerous assistants as they anxiously inquired what they might have the pleasure of showing him. He and Sophia had been there since mid-day; and she had sat in judgment upon carpets which were brought out, plunging like unbroken colts, by panting foremen, and unrolled before her in a blinding riot of colour. Peter had only to express the mildest commendation of any carpet to seal that carpet's doom instantly; so that he soon abstained from personal interference.

Now Sophia was in the ironmongery department, choosing kitchen utensils, and his opinion being naturally of no value on such matters, he was free to roam wherever he pleased within the limits of the building. He felt tired and rather faint, for he had had no lunch; and presently he came to a series of show-rooms fitted up as rooms in various styles: there was one inviting-looking interior, with an elaborate chimneypiece which had cosy cushioned nooks on either side of the fireplace, and into one of these corners he sank with heartfelt gratitude; for it was a comfortable seat, and he had not sat down for hours. But as his weariness wore away, he felt the want of something to occupy his mind, and searched in his pockets to see if he had any letters there—even notes of congratulation upon his approaching marriage would be better than nothing in his present reduced condition. But he had left all his correspondence at his chambers. The only document he came upon was the identical time cheque he had drawn long ago: it was creased and rumpled; but none the less negotiable, if he could find a clock. And on the built-up chimneypiece there was a clock, a small faience affair surmounted by a Japanese monster in peacock-blue. Moreover, by some chance, this clock was actually going—he could hear it ticking as he sat there. Should he present his cheque or not? He was feeling a little aggrieved at Sophia's treatment of him, she had snubbed him so unmercifully over the carpets; it was pleasant to think that, if he chose, he could transport himself that very instant to the society of a sweet and appreciative companion from whom snubbing was the last thing to be apprehended.

Yes; Sophia's treatment quite justified him in making an exception to the rule he had laid down for himself—he would present that cheque. And he rose softly from his seat and pushed the cheque under the little timepiece....

As before, his draft was honoured immediately: he found himself on a steamer-chair in a sheltered passage between two of the deck-cabins. It was night, and he could not clearly distinguish any objects around him for some little time, owing to the darkness; but from a glimmer of white drapery that was faintly visible close by, he easily inferred that there was another chair adjoining his, which could only be occupied by Miss Tyrrell. He could just hear the ship's band playing a waltz at the further end of the ship; it was one of the evenings when there had been dancing, and he and Miss Tyrrell were sitting out together.

All this he realised instantly, and not without a thrill of interest and expectation, which, however, the first words she uttered were sufficient to reduce to the most prosaic perplexity.

"What have I said?" she was moaning, in a voice hardly recognisable from emotion and the fleecy wrap in which her face was muffled,—"oh! what have I said?"

Peter was naturally powerless to afford her any information on this point, even if she really required it; he made a rapid mental note to the effect that their intimacy had evidently made great progress since their last interview.

"I'm afraid," he said, deciding that candour was his only course, "I can't exactly tell you what you did say; for, as a matter of fact, I didn't quite catch it."

"Ah! you say that to spare me," she murmured: "you must have heard; but, promise me you will forget it?"

"Willingly," said Peter, with the greatest readiness to oblige; "I will consider it forgotten."

"If I could but hope that!" she said. "And yet," she added, recklessly, "why should I care what I say?"

"To be sure," agreed Tourmalin at random, "why should you, you know?"

"You must have seen from the first that I was very far from being happy?"

"I must confess," said Peter, with the air of a man whom nothing escaped, "that I did observe that."

"And you were right! Was it unnatural that I should be nothing but grateful to the chance which first brought us together?"

"Not at all," said Peter, delighted to feel himself on solid ground again; "indeed, if I may speak for myself, I have even greater reason to feel grateful to that monkey."

"To what monkey?" she exclaimed.

"Why, naturally, my dear Miss Tyrrell, to the animal which was the unconscious instrument in making us acquainted. You surely cannot have forgotten already that it was a monkey?"

She half rose with an impetuous movement, the mantilla fell from her face, and, even in the faint starlight, he could perceive that, beautiful as that face undoubtedly was, it was as certainly not the face of Miss Tyrrell!

"You seem to have forgotten a great deal," she retorted, with a suppressed sob in her voice, "or you would at least remember that my name is Davenport. Why you should choose to call me Miss Tyrrell, whom I don't even know by sight, I can't conceive!"

Here was a discovery, and a startling one! It appeared that he had not merely one, but two dear friends on board this P. and O. steamer; and the second seemed, if possible, even dearer than the first! He must have made the very most of those extra hours!

There was one comfort, however, Miss Davenport did not, contrary to his impression, know Miss Tyrrell; so that they need not necessarily clash—still, it was undeniably awkward. He had to get out of his mistake as well as he could, which was but lamely.

"Why, of course," he protested, "I know you are Miss Davenport. Most stupid of me to address you as Miss Tyrrell! The—the only explanation I can offer is, that before I had the pleasure of speaking to you, I was under the impression that your proper name was Tyrrell, and so it slipped out again just then from habit."

This—though the literal, if not the moral, truth—did not seem to satisfy her entirely.

"That may be so," she said, curtly; "still, it does not explain why you should address me as Miss Anybody, after asking and receiving permission, only last night, to call me by my Christian name!"

Obviously, their relations were even closer than he had imagined. He had no idea they had got as far as Christian names already, any more than he had of what hers might happen to be.

There was a painful want of method in the manner this Time Bank conducted its business, as he could not help remarking to himself; however, Peter, perhaps from the very timidity in his character, developed unexpected adroitness in a situation of some difficulty.

"So you did!" he said. "You allowed me to call you by your—er—Christian name; but I value such a privilege too highly to use it—er—indiscriminately."

"You are very strange to-night!" she said, with a plaintive and almost childish quiver of the lip. "First you call me 'Miss Tyrrell' then 'Miss Davenport,' and then you will have it that we were introduced by a monkey! As if I should ever allow a monkey to introduce anybody to me! Is saving a girl's life such an ordinary event with you, that you forget all about such a trifle?"

This last sentence compensated Peter for all that had gone before. Here was a person whose life he really had saved; and his heart warmed to her from that moment. Rescuing a girl from imminent bodily peril was a more heroic achievement than capturing the most mischievous of monkeys; and, besides, he felt it was far more in his style. So it was in his best manner he replied to her question:

"It would be strange, indeed," he said, reproachfully, "if I could ever forget that I was the humble means of preserving you from—from a watery grave"—(he risked the epithet, concluding that on a voyage it could hardly be any other description of grave; and she did not challenge it, so he continued)—"a watery grave; but I had hoped you would appreciate the motive which restrained me from—er—seeming to dwell upon such a circumstance."

This appeal, unprincipled as it was, subdued her instantly.

"Oh, forgive me!" she said, putting out her hand with the prettiest penitence. "I might have known you better than that. I didn't mean it. Please say you forgive me, and—and call me Maud again!"

Relief at being supplied with a missing clue made Peter reckless; indeed, it is to be feared that demoralisation had already set in; he took the hand she gave him, and it did not occur to him to let it go immediately.

"Maud, then," he said obediently; "I forgive you, Maud."

It was a prettier name to pronounce than Sophia.

"How curious it is," she was saying, dreamily, as she nestled comfortably in her chair beside him, "that, up to the very moment when you rushed forward that day, I scarcely gave your existence a thought! And now—how little we ever know what is going to happen to us, do we?"

["Or what has happened, for that matter!" he thought.] This time he would not commit himself to details until he could learn more about the precise nature of his dauntless act, which he at once proceeded to do.

"I should very much like to know," he suggested, "what your sensations were at that critical moment."

"My sensations? I hardly know," she said. "I remember leaning over the—bulwarks, is it?" (Peter said it was bulwarks)—"the bulwarks, watching a sailor in a little balcony below, who was doing something with a long line—"

"Heaving the lead," said Peter; "so he was—go on!"

He was intensely excited; it was all plain enough: she had lost her balance and fallen overboard; he had plunged in, and gallantly kept her above water till help arrived. He had always known he was capable of this sort of thing; now he had proved it!

"—When all at once," she continued, "I felt myself roughly dragged back by somebody—that was you! I was rather angry for the moment, for it did seem quite a liberty for a total stranger to take,—when, that very instant, I saw the line with a great heavy lump of lead at the end of it whirled round exactly where my head had been, and then I knew that I owed my life to your presence of mind!"

Peter was more than disappointed—he was positively disgusted at this exceedingly tame conclusion; it did seem hard that, even under conditions when any act of daring might have been possible to him, he could do nothing more brilliant than this. It was really worse than the monkey business!

"I'm afraid you make too much of the very little I did," he said.

"Do I? Perhaps that is because if you had not done it, we should never have come to know one another as we do!" (So far, it was a very one-sided sort of knowledge, Peter thought.) "And yet," she added, with a long-drawn sigh, "I sometimes think that we should both be happier if we never had known one another; if you had stood aside, and the lead had struck me, and I had died!"

"No, no!" said Peter, unfeignedly alarmed at this morbid reflection, "you mustn't take such a gloomy view of it as all that, you know!"

"Why not?" she said, in a sombre tone. "It is gloomy—how gloomy I know better than you!" ("She might well do that," thought Tourmalin.) "Why did I not see that I was slowly, imperceptibly drifting—drifting?"

"Well," said Peter, with a levity he was far from feeling, "if the drifting was imperceptible, you naturally wouldn't see it, you know!"

"You might have spared a joke at such a time as this!" she cried, indignantly.

"I—I wasn't aware there was a close time for jokes," he said, humbly; "not that it was much of a joke!"

"Indeed it was not," she replied. "But oh, Peter, how we have both drifted!"

"Have we?" he exclaimed, blankly. "I—I mean—haven't we?"

"I was so blind—so wilfully, foolishly blind! I told myself we were friends!"

"Surely we are?" he said, retaking possession of her hand; he had entirely forgotten Sophia in the ironmongery department, at Tottenham Court Road. "I—I understood we were on that footing?"

"No," she said; "let us have no subterfuges any more—we must look facts in the face. After what we have both said to-night, we can no longer deceive ourselves by words.... Peter," she broke off suddenly, "I am going to ask you a question, and on your answer my fate—and yours too, perhaps—will depend! Tell me truthfully...." Her voice failed her for the moment, as she bent over towards him, and clutched his arm tightly in her excitement; her eyes shone with a wild, intense eagerness for his reply.... "Would you—" she repeated....

"Would you have the bottle-jack all brass, or japanned? The brass ones are a shilling more."

Peter gave a violent start, for the voice in which this most incongruous and irrelevant question was put was that of Sophia!

Miss Davenport with her hysterical appeal, the steamer-chairs, and the starlight, all had fled, and he stood, supporting himself limply by the arm of the chimney-nook in the upholsterer's showroom, staring at Sophia, who stood there, sedate and practical, inviting his attention to a couple of bottle-jacks which an assistant was displaying with an obsequious smile: the transition was rather an abrupt one.

"Oh, I think the brass one is very nice," he stammered, feebly enough.

"Then that settles it," remarked Sophia; "we'll take the japaned one, please," she said to the assistant.

"Aren't you feeling well, Peter dear?" she asked presently, in an undertone. "You look so odd!"

"Quite well," he said; "I—ah!—was thinking of something else for the moment, and you startled me, that's all."

"You had such a far-away expression in your eyes," said Sophia, "and you did jump so when I spoke to you; you should really try to conquer that tendency to let yourself wander, Peter."

"I will, my love," he said; and he meant it, for he had let himself wander farther than he quite intended.

CHAPTER III

The Third Cheque

As the reader may imagine, this second experience had an effect upon Peter that was rather deterrent than encouraging.

It was a painful piece of self-revelation to find that, had he chosen to avail himself of the extra hours on board the Boomerang as they occurred, he would have so employed them as to place himself in relations of considerable ambiguity towards two distinct young ladies. How far he was committed to either, or both, he could not tell; but he had an uneasy suspicion that neither of them would have been quite so emotional had he conducted himself with the same prudence that had marked his behaviour throughout the time which he was able to account for.

And yet his conscience acquitted him of any actual default; if he had ever really had any passages at all approaching the sentimental with either Miss Tyrrell or Miss Davenport, his mind could hardly be so utterly blank on the subject as it certainly was. No; at the worst, his failings were only potential peccadillos, the kind of weaknesses he might have given way to if he had not wisely postponed the hours in which the occasions were afforded.

He had had a warning, a practical moral lesson which had merely arrived, as such things often do, rather after date.

But, so far as it was possible to profit by it, he would: at least, he would abstain from making any further inroads upon the balance of extra time which still remained to his credit at the bank; he would draw no further cheques; he would return to that P. and O. steamer no more. For an engaged man whose wedding-day was approaching by leaps and bounds, it was, however innocent, too disturbing and exciting a form of distraction to be quite safely indulged in.

The resolution cost him something, nevertheless. Peter was not a man who had hitherto been spoilt by feminine adoration. Sophia was fond of him, but she never affected to place him upon any sort of pinnacle; on the contrary, she looked down upon him protectingly and indulgently from a moral and intellectual pedestal of her own. He had not objected to this, in fact he rather liked it, but it was less gratifying and stimulating to his self-esteem than the romantic and idealising sentiments which he had seemingly inspired in two exceedingly bewitching young persons with whom he felt so much in sympathy. It was an agreeable return from the bread-and-butter of engaged life to the petits fours of semi-flirtation. After all, Peter was but human, and a man is seldom esteemed for being otherwise. He could not help a natural regret at having to abandon experiences which, judging from the fragmentary samples he had obtained, promised so much and such varied interest. That the interest was not consecutive, only made it the more amusing,—it was a living puzzle-picture, the pieces of which he could fit together as he received them. It was tantalising to look at his cheque-book and feel that upon its leaves the rest of the story was written, but that he must never seek to decipher it: it became so tantalising, that he locked the cheque-book up at last.

But already some of the edge had worn off his resolution, and he had begun to see only the more seductive side of interviews which, at the time, had not been free from difficulty and embarrassment. Having put himself beyond the reach of temptation, he naturally began to cast about for some excuse for again exposing himself to it.

It was the eve of his wedding-day; he was in his chambers for the last time, and alone, for he would not see Sophia again until he met her in bridal array at the church door, and he had no bachelor friends whom he cared to invite to help him to keep up his spirits.

Peter was horribly restless and nervous; he needed a sedative of some kind, and even trying on his wedding garments failed to soothe him, as he felt almost certain there was a wrinkle between the shoulders, and it was too late to have it altered.

The idea of one more visit to the Boomerang,—one more interview, the last, with one or other of his amiable and fascinating friends—it did not matter very much which,—presented itself in a more and more attractive light. If it did nothing else, it would provide him with something to think about for the rest of the evening.

Was it courteous, was it even right, to drop his friends without the slightest apology or explanation? Ought he not, as a gentleman and a man of honour, to go back and bid them "Good-bye"? Peter, after carefully considering the point, discovered that it was clearly his duty to perform this trifling act of civility.

As soon as he had settled that, he got out his cheque-book from the despatch-box, in which he had placed it for his own security, and, sitting down just as he was, drew another fifteen minutes, and cashed them, like the first, at the ormolu clock....

This time he found himself sitting on a cushioned bench in the music-room of the Boomerang. It was shortly after sunset, as he could tell from the bar of dusky crimson against the violet sea, which, framed in the ports opposite, rose and sank with each roll of the ship. There was a swell on, and she rolled more than he could have wished.

As he expected, he was not alone; but, as he had not expected, his companion was neither Miss Tyrrell nor Miss Davenport, but a grim and portly matron, who was eyeing him with a look of strong disfavour, which made Peter wish he had not come. "What," he wondered, "was he in for now?" His uneasiness was increased as he glanced down upon his trousers, which, being new and of a delicate lavender tint, reminded him that in his impatience he had come away in his wedding garments. He feared that he must present rather an odd appearance on board ship in this festal attire; but there he would have to stay for the next quarter of an hour, and he must make the best of it.

"I repeat, Mr. Tourmalin," said the matron, "you are doubtless not unprepared for the fact that I have requested a few minutes' private conversation with you?"

"Pardon me," said Peter, quaking already at this alarming opening, "but I am—very much unprepared." "Surely," he thought, "this could not be another dear friend? No, that was too absurd—he must have drawn the line somewhere!"

"Then permit me to enlighten you," she said raspingly. "I sent for you, at a time when we are least likely to be interrupted, to demand an explanation from you upon a very delicate and painful matter which has recently come to my knowledge."

"Oh!" said Peter—and nothing more. He guessed her purpose at once: she was going to ask him his intentions with regard to her daughter! He could have wished for some indication as to whether she was Lady Tyrrell or Mrs. Davenport; but, as he had none at present, "Oh" seemed the safest remark to make.

"Life on board a large passenger-ship, Mr. Tourmalin," she went on to observe, "though relaxed in some respects, is still not without decencies which a gentleman is bound to respect."

"Quite so," said Peter, unable to discover the bearings which lay in the application of this particular observation.

"You say 'Quite so'; but what has your behaviour been, sir?"

"That," said Peter, "is exactly what I should like to know myself!"

"A true gentleman would have considered the responsibility he incurred by giving currency to idle and malicious gossip!"

His apprehensions were correct then: it was one of the young ladies' mothers—but which?

"I can only assure you, madam," he began, "that if unhappily I have—er—been the means of furnishing gossip, it has been entirely unintentional."

She seemed so much mollified by this, that he proceeded with more confidence:

"As to anything I may have said to your daughter—" when she almost bounded from her seat with fury.

"My daughter, sir! Do you mean to sit there and tell me that you had the audacity to so much as hint of such a thing to my daughter, of all people?"

"So—so much depends on who your daughter is!" said Peter, completely losing his head.

"You dared to strike this cruel and unmanly blow at the self-respect of a sensitive girl—to poison her defenceless ears with your false, dastardly insinuations—and you can actually admit it?"

"I don't know whether I can admit it or not yet," he replied. "And—and you do put things so very strongly! It is like this: if you are referring to any conversation I may have had with Miss Tyrrell—"

"Miss Tyrrell? You have told her too!" exclaimed this terrible old matron, thereby demonstrating that, at least, she was not Lady Tyrrell.

"I—I should have said Miss Davenport," said Peter, correcting himself precipitately.

"Miss Davenport as well? Upon my word! And pray, sir, may I ask how many other ladies on board this ship are in possession of your amiable confidences?"

He raised his hands in utter despair.

"I can't say," he groaned. "I don't really know what I may have said, or whom I may have said it to! I—I seem to have done so much in my spare time, but I never meant anything!"

"It may be so," she said; "indeed, you hardly seem to me accountable for your actions or you would not appear in such a ridiculous costume as that, with a sprig of orange-blossom in your button-hole and a high hat, too!"

"I quite feel," said Peter, blushing, "that such a costume must strike you as inappropriate; but—but I happened to be trying them on, and—rather than keep you waiting—"

"Well, well, sir, never mind your costume—the question is, if you are genuinely anxious to repair the wrong you have done, what course do you propose to take?"

"I will be perfectly frank with you, madam," said Peter: "I am not in a position to repair any wrong I have done—if I have done any wrong (which I don't admit)—by taking any course whatever!"

"You are not!" she cried. "And you tell me so to my face?"

After all, reflected Peter, why should he be afraid of this old lady? In a few more minutes he would be many hundreds of miles away, and he would take very good care not to come back again. He felt master of the situation, and determined to brazen it out.

"I do, madam!" he said, crossing his legs in an easy fashion, "Look at it from a reasonable point of view. There is safety in numbers; and if I have been so unfortunate as to give several young ladies here an entirely erroneous impression, I must leave it to you to undeceive them as considerately but distinctly as you can. For me to make any selection would only create ill-feeling among the rest; and their own good sense will show them that I am forbidden by the laws of my country, which I am the last person to set at defiance,—that I am forbidden (even if I were free in other respects, which I am not) to marry them all!"

"The only possible explanation of your conduct is, that you are not in your right mind!" she said. "Who in the world spoke or dreamed of your marrying any one of them? Certainly not I!"

"Oh!" said Peter, hopelessly fogged once more. "I thought I might unintentionally have given them grounds for some such expectation. I'm very glad I was mistaken. You see, you must really make allowances for my utter ignorance—"

"If this idiotic behaviour is not a mere feint, sir, I can make allowances for much; but, surely, you are at least sufficiently in your proper senses to see how abominably you have behaved?"

"Have I?" said Peter, submissively. "I don't wish to contradict you, if you say so, I'm sure. And, as I have some reason to believe that my stay on board this ship will not last very much longer, I should like before I go to express my very sincere regret."

"There is an easy way of proving your sincerity, sir, if you choose to avail yourself of it," she said. "I find it very difficult to believe, from the evident feebleness of your intellect, that you can be the person chiefly responsible for this scandal. Am I correct in my supposition?"

"You are, madam," said Peter. "I should never have got myself into such a tangle as this, if I had not been talked over by Mr. Perkins. I don't know if I can succeed in making myself clear, for the whole business is rather complicated; but I can try to explain it, if you will only have a little patience."

"You have said quite enough," she said. "I know all I wish to know now. So it was Mr. Perkins, who has been using you as his instrument, was it?"

"Certainly," said Peter; "but for him, nothing of this would have happened."

"You will have no objection to repeating that statement, should I call upon you to do so?"

"No," said Peter, who observed with pleasure that her wrath against himself was almost entirely moderated; "but you will have to call soon, or I shall have gone. I—I don't know if I shall have another opportunity of meeting Mr. Perkins; but if I did, I should certainly tell him that I do not consider he has treated me quite fairly. He has put me in what I may call a false position, in several false positions; and if I had had the knowledge I have now, I should have had nothing to do with him from the first. He entirely misled me over this business!"

"Very well, sir," she said; "you have shown a more gentlemanly spirit, on the whole, than I expected. I am glad to find that your evil has been wrought more by want of thought than heart. It will be for you to complete your reparation when the proper time arrives. In the meantime, let this be a warning to you, sir, never to—" ...

But here Peter made the sudden discovery that he was no longer in the music-room of the Boomerang, but at home in his old easy-chair by his bachelor fireside.

"Phew!" he muttered to himself, "that was a bad quarter of an hour while it lasted! What an old she-dragon it was! But she's right—it is a warning to me. I mustn't—I really must not draw any more of these confounded time cheques. I've made that ship too hot to hold me already! I'd better remain for ever in contented ignorance of how I spent that extra time, than go on getting into one mess after another like this! It was a wonder I got out of this one as well as I did; but evidently that old woman knew what Perkins is, and saw I wasn't to blame. Now she'll explain the whole affair to all those girls (whoever they may be), and pitch into Perkins—and serve him right! I'm out of it, at any rate; and now, thank goodness, after to-morrow I shall have nothing to do but live contentedly and happily with dearest Sophia! I'd better burn this beastly cheque-book—I shall never want it again!"

It would have been well for Peter if he had burnt that cheque-book; but when it came to the point, he could not bring himself to destroy it. After all, it was an interesting souvenir of some very curious, if not unique, experiences; and, as such, he decided to preserve it.

CHAPTER IV

The Fourth Cheque

Peter Tourmalin enjoyed his honeymoon extremely, in a calm, sober, and rational manner. Sophia discouraged rapture; but, on the other hand, no one was better fitted to inspire and sustain an intelligent interest in the wonders of Geology; and, catching her scientific enthusiasm, Peter spent many happy hours with her along the cliffs, searching for fossil remains. In fact, the only cloud that threatened to mar their felicity at all was an unfortunate tendency on his part to confuse a trilobite with a graptolite, a blunder for which Sophia had no tolerance. He was hazy about his periods, too, until she sent up to town for Lyell's great work on the subject as a birthday surprise for him, and he read it aloud to her on the sands. Altogether, it was a peaceful, happy time.

And never once in the whole course of his honeymoon did he seriously entertain the possibility of making any further use of his book of blank Time Cheques. If he had contemplated it, no harm would have been done, however, as the book was lying amongst his neglected papers at his former chambers.

He felt no poignant regret when the month came to an end, and they returned to town to take possession of their Marylebone flat: for what was it but shifting the scene of their happiness? And after this had taken place, Peter was still too much occupied to have leisure for idle and mischievous thoughts. Marrying Sophia was, indeed, like loving Sir Richard Steele's fair lady, "a liberal education;" and Peter enjoyed the undivided benefit of her rare talent for instruction.

He had been giving his attention to Astronomy of late, an unguarded remark of his having betrayed to Sophia the extreme crudity of his ideas respecting that science, and she had insisted upon his getting a popular primer, with diagrams, and mastering it as a preliminary to deeper study.

One evening he was in the smaller room of the two that, divided by an arch, served for study and drawing-room combined; and he was busily engaged in working out a simple practical illustration, by the aid of one of the aforesaid diagrams. The experiment required a lamp, a ball of cotton, and an orange transfixed by a knitting-needle, and it had something to do with the succession of the seasons, solar and lunar eclipses, and the varying lengths of day and night on different portions of our globe, though he was not very clear what.

"Don't you find you understand the inclination of the moon's orbit to the plane of the ecliptic better now?" said Sophia, as she came through the arch.

"I think I shall, as soon as I can get the moon to keep steadier," he said, with more hope than he felt; "and it's rather hard to remember whereabouts I am supposed to be on this orange."

"I must get you something to make that clearer," she said; "and you haven't tilted the orange nearly enough. But leave it for a moment; I've brought you in this packet of letters and things the people at your old rooms have just sent down. I wish, while I am away—I shall be back in a minute,—you would just run over them, and tell me if there are any papers you want kept, or if they may all be burnt."

While she was gone, he undid the string which fastened the packet, and found, at the bottom of a mass of bills and documents of no value, the small oblong cheque-book which he had vowed never to see again. Somehow, as his eyes rested on its green cover, the old longing came upon him for a complete change of air and scene. He felt as if he must get away from that orange: there were no lamps but electric lights, and no oranges, on board the Boomerang.

But then, his last visit had not turned out a success: what if he were to find he had drawn another quarter of an hour with that irate matron of the music-room?

However, he had left her, as he remembered, in a comparatively pacific mood. She understood him better now; and besides, thanks to the highly erratic system (if there was any system) on which the payments were made, the chances were immensely against his coming across the same old lady twice running. He thought he would risk that.

It was much more likely that he would meet Miss Tyrrell or Miss Davenport, or it might even be another person to whom he was unconsciously allied by the bond of dear friendship. The only question was, how far he could trust himself in such companionship. But here he felt himself guilty of a self-distrust that was unworthy of him. If, on the two previous occasions, he could not call to mind that he had entertained any deeper sentiment for either young lady than a cordial and sympathetic interest, was it likely that, now he was a married man, he would be more susceptible? He was as devoted to his Sophia as ever, but the wear and tear of several successive evenings spent in elementary Astronomy were telling upon his constitution. Such high thinking did not agree with him: he wanted a plainer mental diet for a change. Fifteen minutes spent in the society of someone with a mind rather less cultivated than his wife's would be very restful. Then, when he came back, he would give his whole mind to the orange again.

In short, all Peter's good resolutions were thrown overboard once more, and he wrote out a cheque for the usual amount in desperate fear lest Sophia might return before he could get it honoured. He felt a certain compunction, even then, in presenting it to the severe and intensely respectable black marble timepiece which recorded the flying hours of his domestic bliss. He almost doubted whether it would countenance so irregular a proceeding; but, although it was on the verge of striking nine, it cashed the cheque without hesitation....

It was mid-day: Peter was sitting on a folding seat, protected from the scorching sun by the awning which was stretched above and along the exposed side of the deck, and, to his great satisfaction, he found Miss Tyrrell reclining in a deck-chair between himself and the railing, and a pleasant picture of fresh and graceful girlhood she presented.

As usual, he was not in time for the beginning of the conversation, for she was evidently commenting upon something he had said.

"How delightful it sounds!" she was saying, "and what a free, unfettered kind of life yours must be, Mr. Tourmalin, from your description!"

Now, this was awkward; because he must have been giving her an airy description of his existence as the bachelor and butterfly he had ceased to be. He answered guardedly, awaiting his opportunity to lead up to a disclosure of the change in his circumstances since they had last met.

"It is pleasant enough," he said. "A little dull at times, perhaps," he added, thinking of the orange.

She laughed.

"Oh, you mustn't expect me to pity you!" she said. "I don't believe you need ever be dull, unless you choose. There must always be friends who are glad to see you."

"I am glad to think," said Peter, "that, when I do feel dull, I have at least one friend—one dear friend—from whom I may count upon a welcome!"

He accompanied this speech with such a look, that she could not well pretend to mistake his meaning; and the next moment he regretted it, for he saw he had gone too far.

"That is a very pretty speech," she said, with a faint flush; "but isn't it a little premature, Mr. Tourmalin, considering that we have scarcely known one another two days!"

For the moment, Peter had forgotten the want of consecutiveness in these eccentric Time Cheques. This interview should by rights have preceded the first he had had with her. He felt annoyed with himself, and still more with the unbusinesslike behaviour of the Bank.

"I—I was anticipating, perhaps," he said. "But I assure you that we shall certainly be friends—I may even go so far as to say, dear friends—sooner or later. You see if I am not right!"

Miss Tyrrell smiled.

"Are you sure," she said, with her eyes demurely lowered—"are you sure that there is nobody who might object to our being on quite such intimate terms as that?"

Peter started. Could she possibly have guessed, and how much did she know?

"There could be nothing for anybody to object to," he said. "Are you—er—referring to any person in particular?"

She still kept her eyes down, but then she was occupied just at the moment in removing a loose splinter of bamboo from the arm of her chair.

"You mustn't think me curious or—or indiscreet, if I tell you," she said; "but before I knew you to speak to, I—I couldn't help noticing how often, as you sat on deck, you used to pull something out of your pocket and look at it."

"My watch?" suggested Peter, feeling uncomfortable.

"No, not your watch; it looked more like—well, like a photograph."

"It may have been a photograph, now you mention it," he admitted. "Well, Miss Tyrrell?" "Well," she said, "I often amuse myself by making up stories about people I meet—quite strangers, I mean. And, do you know, I made up my mind that that photograph was the portrait of someone—some lady you are engaged to. I should so much like to know if I was right or not?"

Here was Peter's opportunity of revealing his real status, and preventing all chance of future misunderstanding. It was not too late; but still it might be best and kindest to break the news gradually.

"You were partly right and partly wrong," he said: "that was the portrait of a lady I was—er—once engaged to."

Unless Peter was very much mistaken, there was a new light in her face, an added brightness in her soft grey eyes as she raised them for an instant before resuming her labours upon the wicker-chair.

"Then you mean," she said softly, "that the engagement is broken off?"

Peter began to recognise that explanation was a less simple affair than it had seemed. If he said that he was no longer engaged but married to the original of that photograph, she would naturally want to know why he had just led her to believe, as he must have done, that he was still a careless and unattached bachelor: she would ask when and where he was married; and how could he give a straightforward and satisfactory answer to such questions?

And then another side of the case struck him. As a matter of fact he was undeniably married; but would he be strictly correct in describing himself as being so in this particular interview? It belonged properly to the time he had made the voyage home, and he was certainly not married then.

In the difficulty he was in, he thought it best to go on telling the truth until it became absolutely impossible, and then fall back on invention.

"The fact is, Miss Tyrrell," he said, "that I can't be absolutely certain whether the engagement is ended or not at this precise moment."

Her face was alive with the sweetest sympathy.

"Poor Mr. Tourmalin!" she said, "how horribly anxious you must be to get back and know!"

"Ah!" said Peter, "yes, I—I shall know when I get home, I suppose."

And he sighed; for the orange recurred once more to his reluctant memory.

"Don't tell me if it pains you too much," she said gently. "I only ask because I do feel so sorry for you. Do you think that, when you do get home, you will find her married?"

"I have every reason for believing so," he said.

"That will be a terrible blow for you, of course?"

"A blow?" said Peter, forgetting himself. "Good gracious me, no! Why should it be? I—I mean, I shall be prepared for it, don't you know!"

"Then it's not so bad after all?" she said.

"It's not at all bad!" said Peter, with a vague intention of loyalty to Sophia. "I like it!"

"I think I understand," she said slowly: "you will not be sorry to find she has married; but she may tell you that she never had the least intention of letting you go so easily?"

"Yes," said Peter, "she may tell me that, certainly"—("if she finds out where I've been," he added, mentally).

"And," she continued, "what would you do then?"

"I suppose," he said—"I suppose I should have to do whatever she wished."

"Yes!" she agreed warmly, "you will do that, even if it costs you something, won't you? Because it will be the only right, the only honourable course to take—you will be the happier for it in the end, Mr. Tourmalin, I am sure you will!"

After all, it seemed to him that she must understand about the Time Cheques—or, why should she urge him to give them up if Sophia demanded such a sacrifice?

"No, I shall not," he said; "I shall miss these times terribly. You don't know what they are to me, or you wouldn't speak like that!"

"Mr. Tourmalin!" she cried, "I—I must not listen to you! You can't possibly mean what you seem to mean. It is wrong—wrong to me, and wrong to her—to say things that—that, for all you know, you are not free to say! Don't let me think badly of you!"

Peter was absolutely horrified! What had he said to agitate her like that? He had merely meant to express the pleasure he found in these brief and stolen visits to the Boomerang; and she had misconstrued him like this! At all hazards, he must explain now, if it took him days to make it clear.

"My dear Miss Tyrrell," he protested earnestly, "you quite misunderstood me—you did, indeed! Pray be calm, and I will endeavour to make my position a little clearer than I'm afraid I have done. The worst of it is," he added, "that the whole thing has got into such a muddle that, for the life of me, I can't exactly make out what my position is at the present moment!"

"You can if you will only recollect that you are this mourning-pin," said a familiar voice; and, with the abruptness characteristic of the Time Cheque system, he was back in his study, staring at the ground glass globe of the lamp and the transfixed orange. The clock behind him was striking nine, and Sophia was offering him a pin with a big black head.

"Oh! am I the mourning-pin?" he repeated, helplessly.

"Really, Peter," said Sophia, "I think the pin, just at this moment, has the more intelligent expression of the two. Do try to look a little less idiotic! Now, see; you stick the pin into the orange to represent your point of view, and then keep on twirling it slowly round."

So Peter twirled the orange slowly round for the remainder of the evening, though his thoughts were far away with Miss Tyrrell. He was wondering what she could have thought of him, and, worse still, what she would think if she could see him as he was employed at that moment?

"I tell you what we must do, Peter,—when you get a little more advanced," said Sophia, enthusiastically, that evening, "we must see if we can't pick up a small secondhand orrery somewhere—it would be so nice to have one!"

"Oh, delightful!" he said, absently.

He was not very clear as to what an orrery was, unless it was the dusty machine that was worked with handles at sundry Assembly-room lectures he had attended in early youth. But of one thing he felt grimly certain—that it was something which would render it necessary to draw more Time Cheques!

CHAPTER V

Periodic Drawings

Whether it was natural sin on Peter's part, or an excusable spirit of revolt against the oppression of an orrery which Sophia succeeded in picking up a great bargain at an auction somewhere, his drafts on the Anglo-Australian Joint Stock Time Bank Limited did not end with the one recorded in the preceding chapter.

And, which was more discreditable still, he no longer pretended to himself that he meant to stop until his balance was completely exhausted. His only care now was to economise, to regulate his expenditure by spreading his drawings over as long a period as possible. With this object he made a careful calculation, and found there were still several hours to his credit; whereupon, lest he should yield to the temptation of drawing too much at any one time, he made out a number of cheques for fifteen minutes apiece, and limited himself to one a week—an allowance which, even under the severest provocation, he rarely permitted himself to exceed.

These weekly excursions, short as they were, were a source of the greatest comfort to him, especially now that he had thrown off any idea of moral responsibility.

By degrees he possessed himself of most of the back-numbers, if they may be so termed, of his dual romance. At one time, he found himself being presented by the grateful Sir William to his daughter; and now that he knew what service he had rendered the Judge, he was less at sea than he would certainly have been otherwise. Another time, he discovered himself in the act of dragging Miss Davenport unceremoniously back from the bulwarks; but here again his memory furnished him with the proper excuse for conduct which, considering that he was not supposed to be acquainted with her, he might have found it difficult to account for satisfactorily. So, after all, there did seem to be a sort of method in the operation of the Time Cheques, arbitrary as it appeared.

One fact that went far to reconcile him to his own conscience was the circumstance that, though the relations he stood in towards both young ladies varied at each interview with the most bewildering uncertainty, so that one week he would be upon the closest and most confidential terms, and the next be thrown back into the conventional formality of a first introduction—these relations never again approached the dangerous level of sentiment which had so alarmed him.

He flattered himself that the judicious attitude he was adopting to both was correcting the false impressions which might have—and for that matter actually had—been given.

He was always pleased to see them again, whichever one it was; they were simply charming friends—frank, natural, unaffected girls—and not too clever. Sometimes, indeed, he recognised, and did his best to discourage, symptoms of a dawning tenderness on their part which it was not in his power to reciprocate.

Peter was in no danger of losing his heart to either; possibly the attractions of each served as a conductor to protect him from the influence of the other. He enjoyed their society, their evident appreciation of all he said and did, but that was all; and as they recognised that there could be no closer bond than that of cordial friendship between them, he was relieved of all misgivings.

Surely it was a blameless and legitimate manner, even for a married man, of spending the idle moments which belonged properly to the days of his bachelorhood! Still, he did not confide this harmless secret of his to Sophia; he might tell her when it was all over, but not so long as her disapproval could affect his plans. And he had an instinct that such a story as he had to tell would fail to appeal to a person of her accurately logical habit of mind.

So, on one occasion when he discovered that he had lost one of the loose cheques he now carried constantly about with him, it was with a feeling very like panic that he reflected that he might have dropped it about the house, where its unusual form would inevitably provoke Sophia's curiosity; and he was much reassured when he was able to conclude, from the fact that she made no reference to it, that he must have lost it out of doors.

It must have been some time after this before his serenity again met with a slight shock: he was walking up and down the deck with Miss Davenport—it happened to be one of the days when he knew her very well indeed.

"Sometimes," she was saying, "I feel as if I must speak to somebody!"

"You know where you will always find a very willing listener!" he said, with a kind of fatherly floweriness that he felt sat well upon him.

"I didn't mean you," she said,—"to some girl of my own age, I meant."

"Oh!" said Peter, "well, that's a very natural feeling, I'm sure. I can quite understand it!"

"Then you wouldn't mind—you wouldn't be angry if I did?" she said, looking up at him with her great childishly serious eyes.

"My dear child," said Peter, getting more fatherly every moment, "how could I possibly object to your speaking to any lady on board if you want to?"

He would have liked to make one or two exceptions, perhaps; but he thought he had better not.

"I am so glad," she said, "because I did—this very morning. I did so want someone to advise me—to tell me what a girl ought to do, what she would do herself in my place."

"Ah!" said Peter, sympathetically, "it is—er—a difficult position for you, no doubt."

"And for you, too!" she said quickly; "remember that."

"And for me too, of course," said Peter, assenting, as he always did now from habit, to anything he did not understand at the moment. "My position might be described as one of—er—difficulty, certainly. And so you asked advice about yours, eh?"

"I couldn't very well help myself," she said. "There was a girl, a little older than I am, perhaps, sitting next to me on deck, and she mentioned your name, and somehow—I hardly know how it came about— but she seemed so kind, and so interested in it all, that—that I believe I told her everything.... You aren't angry with me, are you, Peter?"

She had been making a confidante of Miss Tyrrell! It was awkward, extremely awkward and annoying, if, as he began to fear, her confidences were of a tender character.

"I—I am not exactly angry," he said; "but I do think you might be more careful whom you speak to. What did you tell her?"

"All!" she said, with the same little quiver in her underlip he had noticed before.

"That is no answer," said Peter (it certainly was none for him). "Tell me what you said?"

"I—I told her about you, and about me ... and—and about him!"

"Oh!" said Peter, "about me, and you, and him? Well, and—and how did she take it?"

"She didn't say very much; she turned very pale. It was rather rough at the time, and I don't think she can be a very good sailor; for before I had even finished she got up and went below, and I haven't seen her since."

"But you told her about 'him'?" he persisted; "and when you say 'him,' I presume you refer to—?"

Here he paused expectantly.

"Of course!" she answered, with a touch of impatience. "Whom else should I be likely to refer to?"

"It's excessively absurd!" said Peter, driven to candour at last. "I—I remember perfectly that you did mention all the circumstances at the time: but I've a shocking memory for names; and, just for the minute, I—I find it difficult to recall where 'he' comes in exactly. Curious, isn't it?"

"Curious?" she said, passionately; "it's abominable!"

"It is," agreed Peter; "I quite admit that I ought to know—only, I don't."

"This is cruel, unmanly!" she said, brokenly. "How could you forget—how can you insult me by pretending that you could forget such a thing as that? It is odious of you to make a—a joke of it all, when you know perfectly well that—"

"My—my dear young lady!" he declared, as she left her speech unfinished, "I am as far from any disposition to be jocular as ever I was in my life. Let me beg you to be a little more explicit. We seem to have got into a trifling misunderstanding, which, I am sure, a little patience will easily put right." ...

"Put right?" said Sophia, behind him. "I was not aware, Peter, that the clock was out of order. What is the matter with it?"

He almost staggered back from the chimneypiece, upon which he had found himself leaning in an attitude of earnest persuasion.

"I—I was only thinking, my love," he said, "that it wanted regulating."

"If it does," said Sophia, "you are hardly the proper person to do it, Peter. The less you meddle with it the better, I should think!"

"Perhaps so, my dear Sophia, perhaps so!" said Peter, sitting down with the utmost docility.

He had narrowly escaped exciting suspicion. It was fortunate that there was nothing compromising in the few words she had overheard, but he must not allow himself to be caught so near the clock again.

He was not a little disturbed by the tenor of this last interview. It was bad enough that in some way he seemed to have seriously displeased Miss Davenport; but, besides that, he could not contemplate without uneasiness the probable effect which her confidences, whatever their exact purport, might have upon Miss Tyrrell. For hitherto he had seen no necessity to mention to one young lady that he was even distantly acquainted with the other. As he never by any chance drew them both together, there seemed no object in volunteering such information.

But this only made him more apprehensive of a scene when his next turn with Miss Tyrrell arrived. Perhaps, he thought, it would be wiser to keep away from the Boomerang for a week or two, and give them all time to calm down a little.

However, he had the moral, or rather the immoral, courage to present a cheque as usual at the end of the next week, with results that were even less in accordance with his anticipations than before.

It came about in this way: He was comfortably seated by the fireplace opposite Sophia in a cosy domesticated fashion, and was reading to her aloud; for he had been let off the orrery that evening. The book he was reading by Sophia's particular request was Ibsen's Doll's House, and it was not the fault of the subject (which interested her deeply), but of Peter's elocution, which was poor, that, on glancing from the text, he found that she had sunk into a profound and peaceful slumber.

It was a chance he had been waiting for all day. He was rather tired of Nora, with her innocence and her macaroons, her tarantella and her taradiddles, her forgery and her fancy dress, and he had the cheque by him in readiness; so he stole on tiptoe to the mantelpiece, slipped the paper under the clock, and was just in time to sink back into his easy-chair, before it turned out to be one of the revolving-seats in the dining-saloon on the Boomerang.

There was a tumbler of whisky-and-seltzer on the table in front of him, and he was sitting in close confabulation with his former acquaintance, Mr. Perkins, the Bank Manager.

"That's precisely what I don't know, sir, and what I'm determined to find out!" were the first words he heard from the latter gentleman, who looked flushed and angry. "But it's a scandalous thing, isn't it?"

"Very," said Peter, rather bored and deeply disappointed; for the Manager was but an indifferent substitute for the companion he had been counting upon. "Oh, very!"

"Have you happened to hear anything said about it yourself?" inquired his friend.

"Not a word!" said Peter, with the veracity he always endeavoured to maintain on these occasions.

"To go and shift a statement of that kind on to my shoulders like that, it's like the fellow's confounded impudence!"

For the moment Peter felt a twinge: could the other be referring to anything he had said himself in the music-room? But the Manager was evidently not angry with him, so it must be some other fellow. Only, Peter decided not to allude to the faulty working of the Time Cheques, as he had half-intended to do. Perkins was not in the mood for remonstrances just then.

"Most impudent, I must say," he replied. "By-the-way," he added carelessly, "what was the statement exactly?"

"Why, God bless my soul, sir!" cried the Manager, with unnecessary vehemence, "haven't I been telling you the whole story? Didn't you just ask me who the fellow was who has brought me into this business?"

"So I did," said Peter, "and—and who was he?"

"Your attention seems very wandering this evening! Why, I told you the old woman wouldn't give me his name."

Peter's alarm returned at this allusion to an old woman: what old woman could it be but the terrible matron whom he had encountered in the music-room? However, it was fortunate that she had not mentioned any names: if Perkins knew that he had put all the blame of his entanglements upon the Manager's broad shoulders, he would certainly consider it an ungrateful return for what was intended as a kindness.

"So you said before," he remarked; "some old women are so obstinate!"

"Obstinate? That's the first sensible remark you've made for a long while!" said his candid friend. "I should think she was obstinate! Why, I talked myself hoarse trying to make that old harridan believe that I was as innocent as an unborn babe of any responsibility for this precious scandal—that I'd never so much as heard it breathed till she told me of it: but it wasn't any good, sir; she would have it that I was the originator!"

("So you were!" thought Peter, though he prudently refrained from saying so.)

"She's going to kick up the dooce's own delight as soon as she meets her brother; and all I could get her to say was that then, and not till then, she would give me an opportunity of having it out with the cowardly villain, whoever he may be, that has dared to lay all this gossip at my door!"

Peter did not quarrel with this arrangement of the old lady's, for he would certainly not be on board the Boomerang when she arrived at Plymouth.

"Ah!" he said, with as much interest as he could display in a subject that did not concern him, "he'll find that unpleasant, I daresay."

"I think he will!" said Mr. Perkins, emphatically. "Unless he retracts his infamous calumny, I—I'll kick him from one end of the ship to the other!"

Involuntarily Peter's eyes sought his friend's boots, which, as he sat in a corner seat with his feet extended, were much in evidence; they were strong, suitable boots, stouter than those generally worn on a sea-voyage, and Peter could not repress a slight shudder.

"From one end of the ship to the other," he repeated; "that—that's rather a long way!"

"Quite long enough for him, though not nearly long enough for me!" said the Manager. "I'll teach him to mix me up in these squabbles, when I find him, sir—when I find him! Here, steward, bring some more of these dry biscuits: you'll have some more, won't you?"

But Peter was not in the vein for dry biscuits at that moment, and the Manager continued:

"By-the-by, you might help me in this if you only will. I want to find out if I can before we reach Gib, who this fellow is, but the less I talk about the affair the better."

"Oh! yes," said Peter. "I—I wouldn't talk about it at all, if I were you."

"No, I daresay you're right—can't be too careful with an old cat like that. Well, what I want you to do is to try and find out—quietly, you know—who this infernal fellow is!"

"Well, I daresay I could do that," said Peter.

"No one would think a mild, innocent-looking little chap like you had any particular motive for asking: you might ask some of the men in the smoking-room, and pick up some clue or other."

"So I might," said Peter,—"good idea!"

"Or, I'll tell you what—you might pump the old lady for me, eh?"

"I don't think I quite care about pumping the old lady," said Peter, "but anything else I'll do with pleasure."

"Thanks," said the Manager; "that's a good fellow. I knew I could depend upon you!"

"You can," replied Peter, "though, I fancy," he added, soothingly,—"indeed, I am sure you will find that the old woman has made a good deal out of nothing at all." ...

"What old woman, Peter?" asked Sophia with drowsy asperity. "Not Mrs. Linden, surely!"

Mrs. Linden! Was that the name of the old she-dragon of the music-room? Why, of course not; he was in his arm-chair by his own fire, reading Ibsen to his wife!

"I don't know, indeed, my love—it may be Mrs. Linden," he answered cautiously.

"Nonsense!" said Sophia, crossly. "She's not meant to be old in the play, and who says 'the old woman has made a good deal out of nothing'? Helmer, or Doctor Rank, or Krogstad, or who? You do read so badly, it's quite impossible to make out!"

"No one says it, my dear Sophia; at least, it's not in my edition of the text. You—you must have imagined it, I think!"

"I certainly thought I heard you read it out," she replied; "but your voice is so monotonous, that it's just possible I dropped off for a minute or two."

"I dropped off myself about the same time," he confessed hypocritically.

"You wouldn't drop off, or allow me to drop off either, Peter," said Sophia, who was now thoroughly awake again, "if you felt a more intelligent interest in the tremendous problem Ibsen has set in this play. I don't believe you realise in the least what the lesson is that he means to teach; now do you, Peter?"

"Well, I'm not sure that I do altogether, my love," he admitted.

"I thought as much! What Ibsen insists upon is, the absolute necessity of one-ness between man and wife, Peter. They must belong to each other, complete each other—they must be Twin Souls. Are you a Twin Soul, Peter?"

"Upon my word, my dear, I can't say!" he replied, in some perplexity. In the present very divided state of his sympathies, he could not help thinking that his Soul was more like a Triplet.

"But think," persisted Sophia, earnestly: "have you shared all your Past with me? Is there nothing you have kept back—no feelings, no experiences, which you confine to your own bosom? When you left me to take that voyage, you promised that nothing should induce you to be more than civil to any woman, however young and attractive, with whom Fate might bring you in contact. I want you to tell me, Peter, whether, when you were returning home on board the Boomerang, you kept that promise or not?"

Fortunately for him, she put her question in a form which made it easy to give a satisfactory and a truthful answer.

"When I was returning home on board the Boomerang," he said, "I did not, to the best of my recollection and belief, exchange two words with any female whatever, attractive or otherwise—until," he added, with a timely recollection that she had come on board at Gibraltar,—"until I met you. You pain me with these suspicions, Sophia—you do, indeed!"

"I believe you, Peter," she said, moved by his sincerity, which, paradoxical as it may sound, was quite real; for his intentions had been so excellent throughout, that he felt injured by her doubts. "You have never told me a falsehood yet; but for some time I have been tormented by a fancy that you were concealing something from me. I can hardly say what gave me such an impression,—a glance, a tone, trifles which, I am glad to think now, had not the importance I invested them with. Ah, Peter, never treat me as Helmer did Nora! Never shut me out from the serious side of your life, and think to make amends by calling me your 'little lark,' or your 'squirrel;' you must not look upon me as a mere doll!"

"My dear Sophia!" he exclaimed, "I should never think of addressing you as either a squirrel or a lark; and anyone less like a doll in every respect, I never met!"

"I hope you will always think so, Peter," she said; "for I tell you frankly, that if I once discovered that you had ceased to trust me, that you lived in a world apart into which I was not admitted, that very moment, Peter, I should act just as Nora did—I should leave you; for our marriage would have ceased to be one in any true sense of the word!"

The mere idea of being abandoned by Sophia made him shiver. What a risk he had been running, after all! Was it worth while to peril his domestic happiness for the sake of a few more conversations with two young ladies, whose remarks were mostly enigmatic, and for whom he was conscious in his heart of hearts of not caring two straws?

"Sophia," he said plaintively, "don't talk of leaving me! What should I do without you? Who would teach me Astronomy and things? You know I don't care for anybody but you! Why will you dwell on such unpleasant subjects?"

"I was wrong, Peter," she confessed,—"indeed, I doubt you no longer. It was all my morbid imagination that led me to do you such injustice. Forgive me, and let us say no more about it!"

"I do forgive you," was his generous reply to this appeal, which, coming from Sophia, was a very handsome apology, "and we will say no more about it."

And, upon the whole, Peter thought he had got out of a particularly tight place with more credit than he had any reason to expect—a conclusion in which the reader, however much he or she may disapprove of his conduct on moral grounds, will probably be inclined to agree with him.

CHAPTER VI

Foil and Counterfoil

It would be more satisfactory to an author's feelings, especially when he is aware that he will be held accountable by an indignant public for the slightest deviation on his hero's part from the narrow path of ideal rectitude—it would be more satisfactory to be able to record that this latest warning had a permanent effect upon Peter Tourmalin's rather shifty disposition.

But an author, even of a modest performance such as this, cannot but feel himself in a position of grave responsibility. He must relate such facts as he has been able to collect, without suppression on the one side, or distortion on the other. It is a duty he cannot and dare not evade, under penalty of forfeiting the confidence of his readers.

Peter Tourmalin did draw more Time Cheques, he did go back to the Boomerang, and it would be useless to assert the contrary. We may be able to rehabilitate him to some extent before this story concludes: at present, we can only follow his career with pain and disapproval.

Some allowances must be made for the peculiar nature of the case. To a person of Peter's natural inclination to the study of psychology, there was a strong fascination in watching the gradual unfolding and revelation of two characters so opposite and so interesting as those of Miss Tyrrell and Miss Davenport. That was the point of view he took himself, and it is difficult to say that such a plea is wholly without plausibility.

Then, too, he was intensely curious to know how it would all end, and he might ascertain that in the very next quarter of an hour he drew; there was absolutely no telling.

As for Sophia's threat, that soon lost all terrors for him. She would abandon him, no doubt, if she ever knew; but who was going to tell her, and how could she possibly discover the truth unaided, especially now that her awakening suspicions had been lulled? His secret was perfectly safe, and he could unravel the tangled thread of the history of his remaining extra hours on board the Boomerang without any other hindrance than that of his own scruples—which practically amounted to no hindrance at all.

So Peter continued to be the slave of his clock and his cheque-book, from the counterfoils of which he was disagreeably surprised to discover that he had drawn more frequently, and in consequence had an even smaller balance left to his credit, than he had supposed.

However, he consoled himself by concluding that one or two cheques had probably been mislaid, and were still unpresented, while he was entitled to some additional time in respect of compound interest; so that he need not stint himself at present. Fifteen minutes a week was not an extravagant allowance; and sooner or later, even with the utmost economy, a day would come when his balance would be exhausted, and his cheques returned from the clock marked "No effects—refer to drawer," or some equivalent intimation.

But that day was still distant, and in the meantime he went on drawing with a light heart.

It was a Saturday evening, the day on which Peter generally presented his weekly cheque; but although it was nearly half-past ten, he had had no opportunity of doing so as yet. He was in the drawing-room, and Sophia was reading aloud to him this time, an article on "Bi-metallism" from one of the reviews; for she had been an ardent Bi-metallist from early girlhood, and she naturally wished to win Peter from his Laodicean apathy on so momentous a subject. He listened with surface resignation, although inwardly he was in a fever of impatience to get back upon the Boomerang, where Miss Davenport had been more interesting than usual on his last visit. But he could hardly rise and slip a cheque under the clock before Sophia's very eyes without inventing some decent pretext for such an action, and Bi-metallism had reduced him to a mental condition which was no longer fertile in expedients.

Suddenly Sophia stopped reading and remarked:

"If I remember right, Professor Dibbs has stated the argument more correctly in his little book on Currency. It would be interesting to compare the two; I'll get it."

As Professor Dibbs's work was apparently on a shelf in the study, Sophia took the lamp into the further room.

"Now's my time!" thought Peter, as he brought out the cheque from his waistcoat-pocket. "I mayn't get such another chance this evening."

Even if Sophia could lay her hand on the volume at once, he would have had his quarter of an hour and be comfortably back long before she could pass the arch which separated the two rooms; for, as we have seen, this instantaneous action was one of the chief recommendations of the Time Cheques.

So he cashed his cheque, and was at once transported to the secluded passage between the deck-cabins, the identical place where he had first conversed with Miss Davenport. He was on the same steamer-chair too, and she was at his side; the wind carried the faint strains of a set of "Lancers" to them; from all of which circumstances he drew the inference that he was going to be favoured with the sequel to the conversation that had been so incongruously broken in upon by Sophia's question respecting the comparative merits of bottle-jacks in the Tottenham Court Road warehouse. This was so far satisfactory, indicating as it did that he was at last, after so much trying back, to make some real progress.

"What I want to know first," Miss Davenport was saying, "is, whether you are capable of facing danger for my sake?"

"I thought," he remonstrated mildly, "that I had already given proof of that!"

"The danger you faced then threatened only me. But, supposing you had to meet a danger to yourself, could you be firm and cool? Much will depend on that."

"I—I think," he answered frankly, "that perhaps you had better not count upon me. I have never been a man to court danger: it might find me equal to it if it came,—or it might not."

He did not mean to give it the opportunity.

"Then we are lost, that is all!" she said, with gloomy conviction. "Lost, both of us!"

Peter certainly intended to be lost if the moment of trial ever arrived. Even now he was resolving, for about the twentieth time, that this positively should be his very last cheque; for he by no means liked the manner in which the situation seemed to be developing.

But, seeing that the danger, whatever it might be, was still far enough off, he thought, very sensibly, that it would be a pity to cloud this last interview by any confession of pusillanimity. Knowing that he would return no more, he could surely afford to treat with contempt any consequences his imprudence might have entailed.

So he laughed, as he said:

"You mustn't conclude that I am a coward because I don't care to boast. On the contrary, I believe I am not exactly deficient in physical courage."

"You are not?" she cried, relieved. "Then—then you would not be afraid to face a desperate man?"

"Not a dozen desperate men, if it comes to that!" said Peter, supported by the certainty that it would not come to so much as half a desperate man.

"Then I can tell you now what I have scarcely dared to think of before. Peter, you will have to reckon with Alfred!"

"Well, I'm not much alarmed at anything Alfred may do!" said Peter, wondering who the deuce Alfred was.

"He will come on board; he will demand an explanation; he will insist on seeing you!" she cried.

"Let him!" said Peter.

"You are brave—braver even than I thought; but, ah! Peter, you don't know what Alfred is!"

Peter did not even know who Alfred was, but he was unmoved.

"You leave Alfred to me," he said confidently, "I'll settle him!"

"But I must tell you all. I—I led you to believe that Alfred would raise no objections; that he would quietly accept facts which it is useless to contend against. He will do nothing of the sort! He is a man of violent passions—fierce and relentless when wronged. In the first burst of fury at meeting you, when he comes on board, he is capable of some terrible vengeance, which nothing but perfect coolness on your part—perhaps not even that—will be able to avert. And I—I have brought this upon you!"

"Don't cry," said Peter. "You see, I'm perfectly calm. I don't mind it. If Alfred considers himself wronged by me—though, what I have ever done to give him any reason for revenging himself by personal violence, I must say I can't conceive—"

She stopped him.

"Ah! you have given him cause enough!" she cried. "What is the use of taking that tone to me?"

"I want to see Alfred's point of view, that's all," said Peter. "What does he complain of?"

"What does he complain of? You ask me that, when—Peter," she broke off suddenly, "there is somebody round the corner listening to us—a woman, I'm sure of it. I heard the rustle of a dress.... Go and see if there is not!"

Go and see, and find himself face to face with Miss Tyrrell, who might faint or go into hysterics: Peter knew better than that.

"It's merely your fancy," he said, soothingly, "Who can be there? They are all at the other end of the ship, dancing. Go on telling me about Alfred. I don't yet understand how I have managed to offend him."

"Are you really so dull," she said, with a slight touch of temper, "that you can't see that a man who thought he was going to meet the woman he was engaged to, and finds she has learnt to care for—for somebody else, is likely, even if he was the mildest man in the world—which Alfred is far from being—to betray some annoyance?"

"No, I see that," said Peter; "but—but he can't blame me. I couldn't help it!"

He said this, although her last speech had opened his eyes considerably: he knew now who Alfred was, and also that, in some moment of madness which was in one of the quarters of an hour he had not yet drawn, he must have placed himself in the position of Alfred's rival.

What was he to do? He could not, without brutality, tell this poor girl that he had not the smallest intention of depriving Alfred of her affections; it was better, and easier too, to humour her for the short time that remained.

"Alfred will not take that as an excuse," she said. "It is true we could neither of us help what has happened, but that will not alter the fact that he is quite capable of shooting us both the instant he comes on deck. Alfred is like that!"

"Well," said Peter, unable to abstain from a little more of such very cheap heroism, "I do not fear death—with you!"

"Say that once more," she said; which Peter very obligingly did. "Oh, Peter, how I admire you now! How little I knew you were capable of going so calmly to your doom! You give me courage. I feel that I, too, can face death; only not that death—it is so horrid to be shot!"

"It would be unpleasant," said Peter, placidly, "but soon over."

"No," she said, "I couldn't bear it. I can see him pointing his revolver—for he always carries one, even at a picnic—first at your head, then mine! No, Peter; since we must die, I prefer at least to do so without bloodshed!"

"So do I," he agreed, "very much."

"You do?" she cried. "Then, oh, Peter! why should we wait any longer for a fate that is inevitable? Let us do it now, together!"

"Do what?" said Peter.

"Slip over the side together; it would be quite easy, no one will see us. Let us plunge arm-in-arm into the merciful sea! A little struggle—a moment's battle for breath—then all will be over!"

"Yes, I suppose it would be over then;" he said; "but we should have to swallow such a lot of salt water first!"

He reflected that, even if he emerged from the agonies of drowning, to find himself Bi-metallising with Sophia, the experience would be none the less unpleasant while it lasted. There really must be some limit to his complaisance, and he set it at suicide.

"No," he said at last; "I have always held that to escape a difficulty by putting an end to one's own life is a cowardly proceeding."

"I am a coward," she said; "but, oh, Peter, be a coward with me for once!"

"Ask me anything else!" he said, firmly, "but not to stoop to cowardice. There is really no necessity for it, you see," he added, feeling that he had better speak out plainly. "I have no doubt that Alfred will listen to reason; and when he is told that, although, as is excusable enough with two natures that have much in common, we—we have found a mutual pleasure in each other's society—there has been nothing on either side inconsistent with the—the most ordinary friendship; when he hears that.... Where are you going?" for she was rising from her chair.

"Where am I going?" she replied, with an unsteady laugh. "Why, overboard, if you care to know!"

"But you mustn't!" he cried, scarcely knowing what he said. "The—the captain wouldn't like it. There's a penalty, I'm sure, for leaving the ship while it's in motion—I've seen it on a notice!"

"There is a penalty for having believed in you," she replied bitterly, "and I am going to pay it!"

She broke away and rushed out upon the deck into the starlight, with Peter in pursuit. Here was a nice result of his philandering, he thought bitterly. And yet, what had he done? How could he help the consequences of follies committed in time he had not even spent yet? However, what he had to do now was to prevent Miss Davenport from leaping overboard at any cost. He would even promise to jump over with her, if that would soothe her, and of course he could appoint some time next day—say, after breakfast,—for the performance.

He ran down the shadowy deck until he overtook a flying female form, whose hand he seized as she crouched against the bulwarks.

"Miss Davenport, if you will only just ..." he began, when, without warning, he found himself back upon his own hearth-rug, holding Sophia firmly by the wrist!

He felt confused, as well he might, but he tried to pass it off.

"Did you find Dibbs On Currency, my dear?" he inquired, with a ghastly smile, as he dropped her hand.

"I did not," said Sophia, gravely; "I was otherwise engaged. Peter, what have you been doing?"

"What have I been doing?" he said. "Why, it's not a minute since you went into the study to get that book; look at the clock and see!"

"Don't appeal to the clock, Peter,—answer my question. How have you been occupied?"

"I've been waiting for you to finish that article on Bi-metallism," he had the hardihood to say. "Deuced well-written article it is, too; so clear!"

"I don't refer to what you were doing here," said Sophia. "What were you doing on board the Boomerang?"

"It—it's so long ago that I really forget," he said. "I—I read Buckle on deck, and I talked with a man named Perkins—nice fellow he was—manager of a bank out in Australia."

"It's useless to prevaricate, Peter!" she said. "What I want to know is, who was that girl, and why should she attempt to destroy herself?"

He could hardly believe his ears.

"Girl!" he stammered. "How do you know that any girl attempted anything of that sort?"

"How do I know, Peter?" said Sophia. "I will tell you how I know. I was on board the 'Boomerang,' too!"

At this awful piece of intelligence, Peter dropped into his arm-chair, speechless and quaking. What would come next he could not tell; but anything seemed possible, and even probable, after that!

CHAPTER VII

The Culminating Cheque

"Before I say anything else," said Sophia, who was still standing upon the hearth-rug, gazing down upon the wretched Peter as he sat huddled up in his chair, "you would probably like to know how I came to follow you to that steamer. It is a long story, but I will tell you if you wish to hear?"

Peter's lips moved without producing any articulate sounds, and Sophia proceeded:

"Some weeks ago," she said, "one afternoon when you had gone out for a walk, I found what seemed to be a loose cheque on the carpet. I knew how carelessly you leave things about, and I picked it up, and found that, though it was like a cheque in other respects, it was rather curiously worded. I could not understand it at all, but it seemed to have something to do with the steamer you came home from Australia in; so, intending to ask you for an explanation when you came in, I thought in the meantime I would put it in some safe place where I should be sure to see it, and I put it behind the clock; and then— oh, Peter!—"

Peter understood. The cheques were all payable to "self or bearer." Sophia had innocently presented one, and it had been paid. If he had only taken "order" cheques, this would not have happened, but it was too late now! He continued to imitate the tactics of that eminent strategist, Brer Rabbit; in other words, he "lay low and said nuffin," while Sophia continued:

"Then, without in the least knowing how I came there, I found I was on a big steamer, and as I walked along, perfectly bewildered, I saw the name Boomerang painted on some fire-buckets, and of course I knew then that that was your steamer. I fancied that perhaps, in some way, you might be on board too, and would explain how this had happened to me. At all events, I decided to find out if you were; and seeing a girl reading on deck, I took a chair near her, and after a few introductory remarks I mentioned your name. The effect upon her was such as to convince me that she felt more than an ordinary interest in you. By degrees I drew from her the whole story of her relations with you: she even asked me—me— for advice!"

So Miss Davenport's confidante had not been Miss Tyrrell after all—but Sophia! If he had only known that before!

"I could not speak to her," continued Sophia, "I felt stifled, stupefied by what I had heard! I could bear no more; and so I rose and left her, and walked down some stairs, and somehow found myself back in our own room again! I was more bewildered than ever. I looked for the cheque, but there was nothing, and soon I was forced to believe that the whole thing was imaginary. Still, I was not wholly satisfied. You may remember how I questioned you one evening when you were reading the Doll's House to me; well, your answers quite reassured me for the time. I told myself that my suspicions were too wildly improbable not to have been a delusion. I was even afraid that my brain must be slightly affected, for I had always prided myself upon having my imagination under thorough control. But by degrees, Peter— by degrees—I began to doubt again whether it was really nothing but fancy on my part. I noticed that your manner was suspiciously odd at times. I discovered that there was one drawer in your secretary that you kept carefully locked. I caught your eye wandering towards the clock from time to time. What I suspected I hardly know; but I felt certain that I should find the explanation of that mystery in the locked drawer. I tried key after key, until I found one that fitted. Oh, I am not at all ashamed of it! Had I not a right to know? There were no letters, nothing but a cheque-book; but that cheque-book proved to me that, after all, I had imagined nothing: all the cheques were the same as the one I found on the carpet! I tore one out and kept it by me, and from that time I watched you closely. I saw how restless and impatient you were this evening, and I was certain that you were intending to use a cheque from that book. You were bent on getting back to the Boomerang, and I was equally determined that, if I could help it, you should not go alone. Only I could not be quite sure how you managed to get there, and at last I hit upon a little device for finding out. There is no such person as Professor Dibbs, Peter; I invented him to put you off your guard. As I passed into the other room with the lamp, I saw you, reflected in the mirror over the study chimneypiece, rise and go to the drawing-room mantelpiece: you had a slip of paper in your hand—a cheque, of course. I had the cheque I tore out hidden in the waistband of my dress; and so, as soon as I saw you slip your cheque behind the clock in the drawing-room, I put my cheque behind the one in the study. I was on the deck at once, and it was dark, but I could hear your voice and another's—round a corner. I held my breath and listened. What I heard, you know!"

Peter shrank up in his chair, utterly confounded by this last vagary on the part of the Time Cheques. He certainly would not have supposed that the mere presentation even of a "bearer" cheque by Sophia would entitle her to the same fifteen minutes he was receiving himself. He could only account for it by the fact that the two cheques were cashed simultaneously at two separate clocks; but even this explanation was not wholly satisfactory.

He found his voice at last:

"Well," he said, "now that you know all, what are you going to do about it, Sophia? I—I would rather know the worst!"

"I will tell you that in good time," she replied; "but, first of all, I want you to tell me exactly how you came to have these cheques, and what use you made of them on previous occasions?"

So, slightly reassured by her manner, which was composed, Peter gave her a plain unvarnished account of the way in which he had been led to deposit his extra time, and the whole story of his interviews with Miss Davenport. He did not mention any others, because he felt that the affair was quite complicated enough without dragging in extraneous and irrelevant matter.

"I may have been imprudent," he concluded; "but I do assure you, Sophia, that in all the quarters of an hour I have had as yet, I never once behaved to that young lady in any capacity but that of a friend. I only went on drawing the cheques because I wanted a little change of air and scene now and then. You have no idea how it picked me up!"

"I saw in what society it set you down, Peter!" was Sophia's chilling answer.

"You—you mustn't think she is always like that," he urged. "It took me quite by surprise—it was a most painful position for me. I think, Sophia, your own sense of fairness will acknowledge that, considering the awkwardness of my situation, I—I behaved as well as could be expected. You do admit that, don't you?"

Sophia was silent for a minute or so before she spoke again.

"I must have time to think, Peter," she said: "it is all so strange, so contrary to all my experience, that I can hardly see things as yet in their proper light. But I may tell you at once that, from what I was able to observe, and from all you have just told me, I am inclined to think that you are free from actual culpability in the matter. It was quite clear that that very forward girl was the principal throughout, and that you were nothing more than an unwilling and most embarrassed accessory."

This was so much more lenient a view than he had dared to expect that Peter recovered his ordinary equanimity.

"That was all," he said. "I am very glad you saw it, my dear. I was perfectly helpless!"

"And then," said Sophia, "I was more than pleased by your firm refusal to commit suicide. What you said was so very sound and true, Peter."

"I hope so," said Peter, with much complacency. "Yes, I was pretty firm with her! By the way," he added, "you—you didn't happen to see whether she really did jump overboard, I suppose?"

"I came away just at the crisis," she said. "I thought you would tell me!"

"I came away too," said Peter. "It doesn't matter, of course; but still I should have rather liked to know whether she meant it or not."

"How can you speak of it so heartlessly, Peter? She may have been trying to frighten you; she is just the kind of girl who would. But she may have been in earnest, after all!"

"You see, Sophia," said Peter, "it doesn't matter whether she was or not—it isn't as if it had ever really happened."

"Not really happened? But I was there; I heard, I saw it—nothing could be more real!"

"At any rate," he said, "it only happens when I use those cheques; and she can't possibly carry out her rash intention until I draw another—which I promise you faithfully I will never do. If you doubt me, I will burn the book now before your eyes!"

With these words he went to the drawer and took out the cheque-book.

"No," said Sophia, "you must not do that, Peter. There is much about this Time Bank that I don't pretend to understand, that I cannot account for by any known natural law; but I may not disbelieve my own eyes and ears! These events that have happened in the extra time you chose to defer till now are just as real as any other events. You have made this girl's acquaintance; you have—I don't say through any fault of your own, but still you have—caused her to transfer her affections from the man she was engaged to, and, being a creature of ill-regulated mind and no strength of character, she has resolved to put an end to her life rather than meet his just indignation. She is now on the very point of accomplishing this folly. Well, badly as she has behaved, you cannot possibly leave the wretched girl there! You must go back at once, restrain her by main force, and not leave her until you have argued her into a rational frame of mind."

Peter was by no means anxious to go back at first.

"It's not at all necessary," he said; "and besides, I don't know if you're aware of it, but with the way these cheques are worked, it's ten chances to one against my hitting off the right fifteen minutes! Still," he added, with an afterthought, "I can try, of course, if you insist upon it. I can take my chance with another fifteen minutes, but that must be the last. I am sick and tired of this Boomerang business, I am indeed!"

Shameful as it is to state, he had altered his mind from a sudden recollection that he would not mind seeing Miss Tyrrell for just once more. He had not drawn her for several weeks.

"No," said Sophia, thoughtfully; "I see your objection—fifteen minutes is not enough, unless you could be sure of getting the successors to the last. But I have an idea, Peter,—if you draw out the whole balance of your time, you can't possibly help getting the right fifteen minutes somewhere or other. I think that's logical?"

"Oh, devilish logical!" muttered Peter to himself, who had reasons, which he could not divulge to her, for strongly disapproving of such a plan.

"The fact is, my dear," he said, "it—it's rather late this evening to go away for any time!"

"You forget," she said, "that, however long you are away, you will come back at exactly the same time you started. But you have some other reason, Peter—you had better tell me!"

"Well," he owned, "I might come across someone I'd rather not meet."

"You are thinking of the man that girl said she had been engaged to—Alfred, wasn't it?"

Peter had forgotten Alfred for the moment; and besides, he was not likely to turn up till the Boomerang got to Plymouth, and he knew his extra hours stopped before that. Still, Alfred did very well as an excuse.

"Ah!" he said, "Alfred. You heard what she said about him? A violent character—with a revolver, Sophia!"

"But you told her you were not afraid of him. I felt so proud of you when you said it. And think, you may be able to bring them together—to heal the breach between them!"

"He's more likely to make a breach in me that won't heal!" said Peter.

"Still, as you said yourself, it isn't as if it was all actually existing. What does it matter, even if he should shoot you?"

"I don't see any advantage in exposing myself to any such unpleasant experiences, even if they are only temporary," he said.

"It is not a question of advantage, Peter," rejoined Sophia; "it is a simple duty, and I'm surprised that you don't see it as such. Whatever the consequences of your conduct may be, you cannot evade them like this; you have chosen to begin, and you must go on! I am quite clear about that. Let me see"—(here she took the cheque-book, and made some rapid calculations from the counterfoils)—"yes, you have two hours and three-quarters at least still standing to your credit; and then there's the compound interest. I will tear out all these small cheques and burn them." Which she did as she spoke. "And now, Peter, sit down and fill up one of the blank ones at the end for the whole amount."

"Do you know, Sophia," said Peter, "it occurs to me that this is just one of those matters which can only be satisfactorily arranged by—er—a woman's tact. Suppose I make the cheque payable to you now—eh?"

"You mean, that you want me to go instead of you?" she asked.

"Well," said Peter, "if it wouldn't be bothering you, my dear, I think perhaps it would be—"

"Don't say another word," she interrupted, "or I shall begin to despise you, Peter! If I thought you meant it seriously, I would go upstairs, put on my bonnet, and go back to mamma for ever. I could not bear to be the wife of a coward!"

"Oh, I'll go!" said Peter, in much alarm. "I said what I did out of consideration, not cowardice. But wouldn't to-morrow do as well, Sophia? It is late to turn out!"

"To-morrow will not do as well," she said: "fill up that cheque to-night, or you will lose me for ever!"

"There!" said Peter, as he scrawled off the cheque. "Are you satisfied now, Sophia?"

"I shall be when I see you present it."

"Er—yes," he said; "oh! I mean to present it—presently. I—I think I'll take a small glass of brandy before I go, my dear, to keep the cold out."

"As you will certainly be in a summer, if not tropical, temperature the next moment," she said, "I should advise you to take nothing of the kind."

"I say," he suggested, "suppose I find she has just jumped overboard—what shall I do then?"

"Do! Can you possibly ask? You will jump after her, of course!"

"It's easy to say 'of course,'" he said; "but I never could swim more than twenty strokes!"

"Swim those twenty then, and let come what will; you will be back all the sooner. But don't stand there talking about it, Peter—go!"

"I'm going," he said, meekly. "You'll sit up for me, Sophia, if—if I'm late, won't you?"

"Don't be absurd!" she said. "You know perfectly well that, as I said before, you won't be away a second."

"It won't be a second for you," he said, "but it will be several hours for me; and goodness only knows what I may have to go through in the time! However," he added, with an attempt to be cheerful, "it may all pass off quite pleasantly—don't you think it may, Sophia?"

"How can I tell? You will only find out by going."

"I'm going, my dear—I'm going at once!... You'll give me just one kiss before I start, won't you?"

"I will give you no kiss till you come back and I hear what you have done," said Sophia.

"Very well," he retorted; "you may be sorry you refused, when it's too late! I may never come back at all, for anything I can tell!"

And, little as he knew it, he spoke with an almost prophetic anticipation of what was to come. Never again was he destined to stand on that heart-hrug!

But he dared not linger longer, as he could see from her expression that she would suffer no further trifling; and he slipped his last cheque under the clock,—with consequences that must be reserved for the next chapter.

CHAPTER VIII

Paid in His Own Coin

Peter found himself below this time, in the broad passage, furnished with seats and tables for writing, which divided the passengers' cabins. Above, he heard a confused stir and bustle of excitement, the trampling of feet, the creaking and rattle of chains, orders shouted in English and Hindustani. From the absence of all vibration, in the vessel, it was evident that she had been brought to. Why?

Peter guessed the cause only too easily: the unhappy Miss Davenport had indeed succeeded in carrying out her rash design. She had jumped overboard, and the captain had stopped the engines and lowered a boat in the hope of picking her up before she sank! And he himself—why was he skulking below like this? He had only too much reason to fear that he must have been a witness of the fatal leap; and, instead of plunging overboard to the rescue as a hero ought, had rushed down here ignominiously.

Had he been observed? Was his connection with the tragedy suspected? Could he venture up on deck and inform himself? He tried, but his nerve failed him, and he sank into one of the chairs in a state of almost unbearable suspense.

Just at this moment, he saw the skirts of a muslin gown appear at the head of the broad companion which led to the dining-saloon. Someone, a girl evidently, was descending. Presently he saw her fully revealed—it was Miss Tyrrell.

Perhaps he had never been so glad to see her before. She was a friend, a dear friend. She, at least, would sympathise with him, would understand that it was not his fault if he had been too late to avert a catastrophe. She was coming to him. Her eyes were friendly and pitiful as they sought his. She, at least, did not turn from him!

"How pale, how terribly pale you look!" she said. "You must nerve yourself to see her—it cannot be long now!"

"Has she been brought on board yet?" he gasped. "Is—is there any hope?"

"We shall know very soon. It is possible you may find that all is at an end."

"Ah! you think so? But—but no one will say it was my fault, will they? I—I was ready to make any sacrifice—only somehow, when the moment comes, I am apt to lose my presence of mind."

"Yes, I know," she said feelingly; "you are not quite yourself yet, but I know you would make the sacrifice if your duty demanded it. But she may have taken advantage of your absence to free herself and you from all obligation, may she not?"

This suggestion comforted Peter.

"She must have done!" he said. "Yes, of course. I could not be expected to prevent it, if I wasn't there; and I wasn't, when it came to the point. But, Miss Tyrrell, do you think that it is really all over? She—she may come round after all!"

"She may—but of course, if it is true that she is engaged to another, she can have no possible claim on you."

What a sensible right-minded way this girl had of looking at things! thought Peter, not for the first time.

"Why, of course she can't!" he cried. "And it is true. She is engaged—to a fellow of the name of Alfred."

"You know that as a fact?" she exclaimed.

"I know it from her own lips, and I need not say that I should be the last person to wish to—er—upset so desirable an arrangement."

"Why—why didn't you tell me all this before?" she inquired.

"I—I didn't think it would interest you," he replied.

Here, to Peter's utter astonishment, she covered her face with her hands.

"Not interest me!" she murmured at last. "Oh, how could you—how could you keep this from me? Can't you see—can't you guess what a difference it has made in my feelings?"

It might be very dull of him, but he could not perceive why the fact of Miss Davenport's engagement to Alfred should affect Miss Tyrrell so strangely as this!

"I may call you 'Peter' now," she said. "Oh, Peter, how happy you have made me! Why did you keep silence so long? It was too quixotic! Don't you understand even yet?"

"No," said Peter blankly, "I'm afraid I don't."

"Then, if you are really so diffident, I—I must tell you that if you were to ask a certain question once more, I might—I don't say I should, but I might—meet it with a different answer!"

"Good heavens!" he ejaculated, involuntarily.

"But you must not ask me yet—not just yet. I must have time to consider. I must tell papa before I decide anything. You will wait a little longer, won't you, Peter?"

"Yes," he said, feeling limp, "I'll wait. I'd rather!"

She smiled radiantly upon him, and then fled lightly up the companion, leaving him with fresh cause for uneasiness. He could no longer doubt that, for some reason, she expected him to propose to her, which it seemed he had already, in one of those confounded extra minutes, been unprincipled enough to do! Now she had gone to inform her father, the Judge, and he would have the disagreeable task of disabusing them before long!

At this point he started, believing that he was visited by an apparition; for a cabin-door opened, and Miss Davenport came out and stood before him.

But she was so obviously flesh and blood—and so dry—that he soon saw that all his anxiety on her account had been superfluous.

"Then you—you didn't jump overboard after all?" he faltered, divided between relief and annoyance at having been made to come back, as it were, on false pretences.

"You know who prevented me, and by what arguments!" she said, in a low strained voice.

"Do I?" he said, helplessly.

"Who should, if you do not? Did not you implore me not to leave you, and declare that, if I would only have courage and wait, we should be happy even yet? And I did wait. For what, I ask you, Peter Tourmalin—for what?"

"It's really no use asking me," he said, "for I've no idea!"

"I waited—to discover that all this time you have had a secret understanding with another; that you are about to transfer your fickle affections to—to that fair girl! Don't deny it, Peter! I was listening. I see it all—all!"

"I wish to goodness I did!" he said. "I never was in such a muddle as this in my life. I can only assure you that if that young lady really imagines that I am, or can be, anything more to her than a friend, she is entirely mistaken. I was just about to go up and explain as much to her father!"

"You are not deceiving me?" she asked, earnestly. "You are sure?"

"I will swear it, if you wish!" he replied.

"No," she said, relenting visibly, "your word is enough. I do believe you, and I am almost happy again. So long as you do not desert me, even Alfred loses half his terrors!"

"Exactly," he said; "and now, if you will excuse me, I'll just run up on deck and settle this other business."

He went up to the hurricane-deck, and found the ship had anchored. In front was a huge barren rock, with lines of forts, walls, and telegraph poles; and at its base, a small white town huddled. They had arrived at Gibraltar, which accounted for the absence of motion.

As he stood there, taking this in, he was accosted by Sir William Tyrrell, who thrust his arm through Peter's in a friendly manner.

"My dear boy," said the Judge heartily, "Violet has just told me the good news. I can only say that I am delighted—most delighted! I have always felt a warm interest in you, ever since that affair of—"

"Of the monkey," said Peter. "I am very glad to hear it, Sir William; but—but I ought to tell you that I am afraid Miss Tyrrell was—a little premature. She misinterpreted a remark of mine, which, in point of fact, referred to somebody else altogether."

"Then you have no more reason than before for assuming that your fiancée has thrown you over. Am I to understand that?"

"No more reason than before," admitted Peter.

"And your uncertainty still continues? Very unsatisfactory, I must say! I do think, my dear fellow, that, in your position, you should have been more careful to refrain from betraying any interest in Violet until you knew that you were free to speak. As it is, you may have cast a shadow upon her young life that it will take years to dispel!"

Peter's heart sank into his boots for very shame at this gentle and almost paternal reproof.

"Yes," continued the worthy Judge, "Violet is a high-minded girl, scrupulously sensitive on points of honour; and, unless the young lady you are under a semi-engagement to should release you of her own free will, I know my daughter too well to doubt that she will counsel you to fulfil your contract and renounce all hope so far as she is concerned."

Peter felt a little easier.

"I—I am prepared to do that," he said.

"Well, I don't say myself that I go quite so far as she does; but strictly, no doubt, a promise is a promise, and should be kept at all hazards. You have done all that a man can honourably do to put himself right. You have written to this young lady, so I understand, informing her of the change in your sentiments, and offering, nevertheless, to redeem your promise if she insisted upon it. I think that was the general purport of your letter?"

Here was one more evil fruit of his extra time! What would Sophia think, or say, or do, if such a letter as that ever came to her knowledge? Fortunately, that at least was impossible!

"You have some grounds," the Judge went on, "for assuming that the lady has already treated the contract as non-existent—a person called Alfred, I think my daughter said?"

"No, that was a mistake," explained Peter. "Alfred is engaged to quite a different person."

"Well, in any case, it is quite possible that you may obtain your release when you meet her; and your suspense will soon be over now. Miss—er—Pincher, is it?—will probably be on board the ship before many minutes. I see the boats are putting out from the harbour already."

"What!" cried Peter, with the terrible conviction darting through his mind that Sir William spoke the bare truth.

Sophia had said something about meeting him at Gibraltar; but if she had done so during the real voyage, how could he have the meeting all over again, with this ghastly variation? If he could only remember whether she had come out, or not! It was singular, incomprehensible! But his memory was a blank on such a vital fact as this!

"Would you like to have my field-glass for a moment?" said Sir William, considerately.

Peter took it, and the next moment the binocular fell from his nerveless hands. He had seen only too clearly the familiar form of Sophia seated in the peaked stern of a small craft, which a Spanish boatman was "scissoring" through the waves towards the Boomerang.

"Come, courage!" said the Judge kindly, as he picked up his glass and wiped the lenses. "Don't be nervous, my boy. You don't know what she may have to say to you yet, you know!"

"No, I don't!" he groaned. "I—I think I ought to go down to the gangway and meet her," he added, tremulously,—not that he had any intention of doing so, but he wanted to be alone.

Before the Judge could even express his approbation of Peter's course, Tourmalin was down on the saloon-deck seeking a quiet spot wherein to collect his thoughts.

Before he could find the quiet spot, however, he almost ran into the arms of the matron from Melbourne, whom he had not seen since the episode of the music-room.

"A word with you, Mr. Tourmalin!" she said.

"I—I really can't stop now," stammered Peter. "I—I'm expecting friends!"

"I, too," she said, "am expecting a relation, and it is for that reason that I wish to speak to you now. My brother, who has been staying at Gibraltar on account of his health, will be as determined as I am to trace and punish the infamous calumny upon the name and career of our honoured parent."

"I daresay, madam," said Peter,—"I daresay. Very creditable to you both—but I really can't stop just now!"

"You appear to forget, sir, that, unless you can satisfactorily establish your innocence, my brother will certainly treat you as the person primarily responsible for an atrocious slander!"

"A slander—upon your father!... Me?" said the indignant Peter. "Why, I never heard of the gentleman!"

"Denial will not serve you now," she said. "I have not only your own admissions in the music-room, but the evidence of more than one trustworthy witness, to prove that you circulated a report that my dear father—one of the most honoured and respected citizens of Melbourne—began his Colonial career as— as a transported convict!"

After all, as the hapless Peter instantly saw, he might have said so, for anything he knew, in one of those still unexhausted extra quarters of an hour!

"If I said so, I was misinformed," he said.

"Just so; and in our conversation on the subject, you mentioned the name of the person who used you as his mouthpiece to disseminate his malicious venom. What I wish to know now is, whether you are prepared or not to repeat that statement?"

Peter recollected now that he had used expressions implicating Mr. Perkins, although merely as the origin of totally different complications.

"I can't positively go so far as that," he said. "I—I made the statement generally."

"As you please," she said. "I can merely say that my brother, whom I expect momentarily, is, although an invalid in some respects, a powerful and determined man; and unless you repeat in his presence the sole excuse you have to offer, he will certainly horsewhip you in the presence of the other passengers. That is all, sir!"

"Thank you—it's quite enough!" murmured Peter, thinking that Alfred himself could hardly be much more formidable; and he slipped down the companion to the cabin-saloon, where he found Miss Davenport anxiously expecting him.

"He is here," she whispered. "I have just seen him through the port-hole."

"What—the old lady's brother!" he replied.

"He has no sister who is an old lady. I mean Alfred."

"Alfred?" he almost yelped. "Alfred here!"

"Of course he is here. Is not his battalion quartered at Gibraltar? You knew it; we were to meet him here!"

"I didn't, indeed—or I should never have come!" he protested.

"Don't let us waste words now. He is here; he will demand an explanation from you. He has his pistol with him—I could tell by the bulge under his coat. We must both face him; and the question is, What are you going to say?"

Peter thrust his hands through his carefully-parted hair:

"Say?" he repeated. "I shall tell him the simple, straightforward truth. I shall frankly admit that we have walked, and sat, and talked together; but I shall assure him, as I can honestly, that during the whole course of our acquaintance I have never once regarded you in any other light but that of a friend."

"And you suppose that, knowing how I have changed, he will believe that!" she cried. "He will fire long before you can finish one of those fine sentences!"

"In that case," suggested Peter, "why tell him anything at all? Why not spare him, poor fellow, at all events for the time? It will only upset him just now. Let him suppose that we are strangers to one another; and you can break the truth to him gently when you reach England, you know. I 'm sure that's much the more sensible plan!"

She broke into strange mirthless laughter.

"Your prudence comes too late," she said. "You forget that the truth was broken to him some days ago, in the letter I wrote from Brindisi."

"You wrote and broke it to him at Brindisi!" cried Peter. "What induced you to do that?"

"Why, you!" she retorted. "You insisted that it was due to him; and though I knew better than you what the effect would be, I dared not tell you the whole truth. I wanted to end the engagement, too; and I scarcely cared then what consequences might follow. Now they are upon us, and it is useless to try to escape them. Since we must die, let us go up on deck and get it over!"

"One moment," he said; "Alfred can wait a little. I—I must go to my cabin first, and put on a clean collar."

And with this rather flimsy pretext, he again made his escape. He made up his mind what to do as he rushed towards his cabin. He could hardly have been anything like an hour on board the Boomerang as yet; he had to get through at least another three before he could hope for deliverance. His only chance was to barricade himself inside his cabin, and steadfastly refuse to come out, upon any consideration whatever, until he was released by the natural expiration of time.

He sped down the passage, and found, to his horror, that he had forgotten the number of his berth. However, he knew where it ought to be, and darted into an open door, which he fastened securely with hook and bolt, and sank breathless on one of the lower berths.

"You seem in a hurry, my friend!" said a voice opposite; and Peter's eyes, unused at first to the comparative dimness, perceived that a big man was sitting on the opposite berth, engaged in putting on a pair of spiked cricket-shoes. He had bolted himself inside the cabin with Mr. Perkins!

CHAPTER IX

Compound Interest

The Bank Manager looked across at Peter with an amused smile; he seemed quite friendly. Whether he was in Peter's cabin, or Peter in his, did not appear; and perhaps it was not of much consequence either way. If the cabin belonged to Mr. Perkins, he did not, at all events, appear to resent the intrusion.

"You seem rather put out about something," he said again, as Peter was still too short of breath for words.

"Oh, no," panted Peter, "it's nothing. There was so much bustle going on above, that I thought I'd come in here for a little quiet; that's all."

"Well," said the Manager, "I'm glad you looked in; for, as it happens, you're the very man I wanted to see. I daresay you're wondering why I'm putting on these things?"

Peter nodded his head, which was all he felt equal to.

"Why, I've just been having a talk with that old she-griffin from Melbourne. Perhaps you don't know that her brother is coming on board directly?"

"Oh yes, I do!" said Peter.

"Well, it seems she means to denounce me to him as the slanderer of her father. She may, if she chooses; my conscience is perfectly clear on that score. No one can bring anything of the sort home to me; and I've no doubt I shall soon satisfy him that I'm as innocent as an unborn babe. Still, I want you, as a respectable man and the only real friend I have on board, to come with me and be my witness that you never heard such a rumour from my lips; and besides, sir, we shall have an opportunity at last of seeing the unutterable scamp who has had the barefaced impudence to say I told him this precious story! She's going to produce him, sir; and if he dares to stand me out to my face—well, he'll know why I've put on these shoes! Come along; I can't let you off."

Peter dared not refuse, for fear of attracting his friend's suspicions. He could only trust to slipping away in the confusion; and so, unfastening the cabin-door, the Manager caught the unresisting Tourmalin tightly by the arm, and hurried him along the central passage and up the companion.

Even Miss Davenport would have been a welcome diversion at that moment; but she was not there to intercept him, and he reached the upper deck more dead than alive.

"Where's that old vixen now?" exclaimed the Manager, dropping Peter's arm. "Here, just stay where you are a minute, till I find her and her confounded brother!"

He bustled off, leaving Tourmalin by the davits, quite incapable of action of any kind in the presence of this new and awful dilemma. He had been spreading a cruel and unjustifiable slander against an irreproachable Colonial magnate, whose son was now at hand to demand reparation with a horsewhip. He could only propitiate him by denouncing Perkins as his informant, and if he did that he would be kicked from one end of the ship to the other with a spiked boot! This was Nemesis indeed, and it was Sophia who had insisted upon his exposing himself to it. What a fool he was not to fly back to that cabin, while he could!

He turned to flee, and as he did so a hand was passed softly through his arm.

"Not that way, Peter!" said Miss Tyrrell's voice.

A wild, faint hope came to him that he might be going to receive one of the back quarters of an hour. The caprices of the Time Cheques were such that it was quite possible he would be thrown back into an earlier interview. Little as he felt inclined for any social intercourse just then, he saw that it would afford him a brief interlude—would at least give him breathing-time before his troubles began again.

"I will go wherever you choose," he said; "I am in your hands."

"I came," she said, "to take you to her. She is asking for you."

"She?" said Peter. "For heaven's sake, who?"

"Why, Miss Pinceney, of course. I knew who it was directly I saw her face. Peter, is it true, as papa tells me, that I misunderstood you just now—that she is not engaged to Alfred?"

"Alfred? No!" he replied. "If she is engaged to anyone at all, I have strong grounds for supposing it's to me!"

"Then we must submit, that is all," said Miss Tyrrell. "But we do not know her decision yet; there is still hope!"

"Yes," he said, "there is hope still. Let us go to her; make haste!"

He meant what he said. Sophia could at least extricate him from a portion of his difficulties. Miss Tyrrell—magnanimous and unselfish girl that she was, in spite of her talent for misapprehension—was ready to resign him to a prior claim, if one was made. And Sophia was bound to claim him; for if the engagement between them had been broken off, he could not now be her husband, as he was. Even Time Cheques must recognise accomplished facts.

He followed her across the ship, turning down the very passage in which he had sat through more than one cheque with Miss Davenport; and on the opposite side he found Sophia standing, with her usual composure, waiting for his arrival.

She was so identically the same Sophia that he had left so lately, that he felt reassured. She, at least, could not be the dupe of all this. She had come—how, he did not trouble himself to think,—but she had come with the benevolent intention of saving him!

"How do you do, my love?" he began. "I—I thought I should see you here."

"You only see me here, Peter," she replied, in a voice that trembled slightly, in spite of her efforts to command it, "because I felt very strongly that it was my duty to put an end at the earliest moment to a situation which has become impossible!"

"I'm sure," said Peter, "it is quite time it was put an end to—it couldn't go on like this much longer."

"It shall not, if I can help it," she said. "Miss Tyrrell, pray don't go away; what I have to say concerns you too."

"No; don't go away, Miss Tyrrell," added Peter, who felt the most perfect confidence in Sophia's superior wisdom, and was now persuaded that somehow it was all going to be explained. "Sir William, will you kindly step this way too? Sir William Tyrrell—Miss Pinceney. Miss Pinceney has something to tell you which will make my position thoroughly clear."

"I have only to say," she said, "that your honourable and straightforward conduct, Peter, has touched me to the very heart. I feel that I am the only person to blame, for it was I who insisted upon your subjecting yourself to this test."

"It was," said Peter. "I told you something would happen—and it has!"

"I would never hold you to a union from which all love on your side had fled; do not think so, Peter. And now that I see my—my rival, I confess that I could expect no other result. So, dear Miss Tyrrell, I resign him to you freely—yes, cheerfully—for, by your womanly self-abnegation you have proved yourself the worthier. Take her, Peter; you have my full consent!"

"My dear young lady," said the Judge, deeply affected, "this is most noble of you! Allow me to shake you by the hand."

"I can't thank you, dear, dear Miss Pinceney!" sobbed his daughter. "Peter, tell her for me how we shall both bless and love her all our lives for this!"

Peter's brain reeled. Was this Sophia's notion of getting him out of a difficulty?

As he gazed distractedly around, his eyes became fixed and glazed with a new terror. A stalwart stranger, with a bushy red beard, was coming towards him, with a stout riding-whip in his right hand. By his side walked the Manager, from whose face all vestige of friendliness had vanished.

"As soon as you have quite finished your conversation with these ladies," said the Manager, with iron politeness, "this gentleman would be glad of a few moments with you; after which I shall request your attention to a little personal affair of my own. Don't let us hurry you, you know!"

"I—I won't," returned Peter, flurriedly; "but I'm rather busy just now: a little later, I—I shall be delighted."

As he stood there, he was aware that they had withdrawn to a bench some distance away, where they conferred with the elderly lady from Melbourne. He could feel their angry glare upon him, and it contributed to rob him of the little self-possession he had left.

"Sophia," he faltered piteously, "I say, this is too bad—it is, really! You can't mean to leave me in such a hole as this—do let's get home at once!"

Before she could make any reply to an appeal which seemed to astonish her considerably, a thin, bilious-looking man, with a face twitching with nervous excitement, a heavy black moustache, and haggard eyes, in which a red fire smouldered, appeared at the gangway and joined the group.

"I beg your pardon," he said, lifting his hat; "forgive me if I interrupt you, but my business is urgent—most urgent! Perhaps you could kindly inform me if there is a—a gentleman" (the word cost him a manifest struggle to pronounce)—"a gentleman on board of the name of Tourmalin? I have a little matter of business" (here his right hand stole to his breast-pocket) "to transact with him," he explained, with a sinister smile that caused Peter to give suddenly at the knees.

"It's that infernal Alfred!" he thought. "Now I am done for!"

"Why," said Miss Tyrrell, who was clinging affectionately to Peter's arm, "this is Mr. Tourmalin! You can speak to him now—here, if you choose. We have no secrets from one another—have we, Peter?"

"I have lately learnt," said the gloomy man, "that a certain Mr. Tourmalin has stolen from me the affection of one who was all heaven and earth to me!"

"Then it must be another Mr. Tourmalin," said Miss Tyrrell, "not this one; because—surely you do not need to be told that you have no rivalry to fear from him?" she broke off, with a blush of charming embarrassment.

Alfred's scowl distinctly relaxed, and Peter felt that, after all, this unfortunate misunderstanding on Miss Tyrrell's part might prove serviceable to him. Since Sophia, for reasons of her own, refused to assist him, he must accept any other help that offered itself.

"The best proof I can give you of my innocence," he said, "is to mention that I have the honour to be engaged to this lady."

He heard a stifled shriek from behind him as he made this assertion, and the next moment Miss Davenport, who must have come up in time to catch the last words, had burst into the centre of the group.

"It is not true!" she cried. "Alfred, you must not believe him!"

"Not true?" exclaimed Alfred, Sophia, Miss Tyrrell, and Sir William, in the same breath.

"No!" said Miss Davenport; "at least, if he has really engaged himself, it is within the last few minutes, and with the chivalrous intention of shielding me! Peter, I will not be shielded by such means. Our love is too precious to be publicly denied. I cannot suffer it; I will acknowledge it, though it costs me my life! You," she added, turning to Sophia,—"you can prove that I speak the truth. It was to you that I confided, that day we met on deck, the story of our fatal attachment."

"I really think you must be mistaken," said Sophia, coldly. "If you confided such a story to anybody, it could not have been to me; for, until a few minutes ago, I had never set foot upon this ship."

How Sophia could stand there and, remembering, as she must do, her recent appropriation of the Time Cheque, tell such a downright fib as this, passed Peter's comprehension. But, as her statement was in his favour so far as it went, he knew better than to contradict it.

"Whether it was you or not," insisted Miss Davenport, "it is he and no one else who rendered my engagement to Alfred utterly repugnant to me! Can you look at him now, and doubt me longer?"

"So, Peter," said Sophia severely, "you could not even be faithful to your unfaithfulness!"

Miss Tyrrell made no comment, but she dropped his arm as if it had scorched her fingers, whereupon Miss Davenport clung to it in her stead, to Peter's infinite dismay and confusion.

"He is faithful!" she cried. "It is only a mistaken sense of honour that made him apparently false. Yes, Alfred, what I wrote to you, and the postscript he added, is the simple truth. We cannot command our own hearts. Such love as I once had for you is dead—it died on the fatal day which brought him across my path. We met—we love; deal with us as you will! I would rather, ever so much rather, die with him than lose him now!"

Alfred was already beginning to fumble fiercely in his breast-pocket. Peter felt the time had arrived for plain speaking; he could not submit to be butchered under a ridiculous misapprehension of this kind.

"Listen to me!" he said eagerly, "before you do anything rash, or you may bitterly regret it afterwards. I do assure you that I am the victim—we are all the victims of a series of unfortunate cheques—I should say, mistakes. It's absurd to make me responsible for the irregular proceedings of a nonsensical Bank. If I had spent my time as I ought to have done at the time, instead of putting it out on deposit, I should never have dreamed of employing it in any kind of philandering!"

"That," said Sophia, "is undeniable: but you spent it as you ought not to have done!"

"Such a speech comes ill from you," he said, reproachfully, "after having expressly condoned the past; and, however I may have appeared to philander, I can conscientiously declare that my sentiments towards both of these young ladies—both, you understand—have been restricted to a respectful and—and merely friendly esteem.... Don't shoot, Alfred!... I thought that was quite understood on all sides. Only have a little more patience, Alfred, and I will undertake to convince even you that I could not for a moment have contemplated depriving you of the hand of this extremely charming and attractive lady, who will not let go my arm.... I—I am a married man!"

"Married!" shrieked Miss Davenport, cowering back.

"Married!" exclaimed Miss Tyrrell, as she hid her face upon her father's shoulder.

"Married!" shouted the Judge. "By heavens, sir, you shall account to me for this!"

"Married!" cried Sophia. "Oh, Peter, I was not prepared for this! When? Where?"

"When? Where?" he echoed. "You were not prepared for it? Perhaps you will ask me next who my wife is!"

"I shall not indeed," said Sophia, "for I have no longer the slightest curiosity on such a subject!"

Peter collapsed upon the nearest bench.

"Sophia?" he cried hoarsely, "why keep this up any longer? Surely it is gone far enough—you can't pretend you don't know!"

But while he spoke the words, he saw suddenly that his attempt to force her hand was hopeless: she was quite sincere in her surprise; she was the Sophia of six months ago, and no amount of explanation could ever make her comprehend what had happened since that time!

And here Alfred broke his silence.

"What you have just confessed," he said, "removes my last scruple. I might, for all I can tell, have stayed my hand and spared your life upon your promise to make Maud happy; for, in spite of her treatment of me, her happiness is still my first consideration. But now you have declared that impossible,—why, as soon as I can get this revolver out of my pocket—for it has stuck in the confounded lining—I will shoot you like a rabbit!"

"Sir William," cried Peter, "I appeal to you! You are the representative of Law and Order here. He is threatening a breach of the Peace—the Queen's Peace! I call upon you to interfere!"

"I am no advocate," said Sir William, with judicial calm, "for taking the law into one's own hands. I even express a hope that this gentleman will not carry out his avowed intention, at least until I have had time to withdraw, and I must not be understood to approve his action in any way. At the same time, I am distinctly of opinion that he has received sufficient provocation to excuse even such extreme measures, and that the fate he threatens will, if summary, at least be richly deserved."

"I think so too," said Sophia, "though it would be painful to be compelled to witness it!"

"Terrible!" agreed Miss Tyrrell. "Let us hide our eyes, dear!"

"Stay, Alfred!" Miss Davenport implored, "have some pity! Think—with all your faults, you are a keen sportsman—you would not shoot even a rabbit sitting! Give Mr. Tourmalin a start of a few seconds—let him have a run before you fire!"

All this time Alfred was still fumbling for and execrating the obstinate weapon.

"I decline to run!" Peter cried from his seat; he knew too well that he could not stir a limb. "Shoot me sitting, or not at all, but don't keep me waiting any longer!"

His prayer seemed likely to be granted, for Alfred had at last succeeded in extricating the revolver; but before he could take aim, the Bank Manager and the Melbourne man ran in and interposed.

"Hold on one minute, sir," they said; "we, too, have business with the gentleman on the seat there, and you will admit that it must be concluded before yours, if it is to be settled at all. We must really ask you to postpone your little affair until we have finished. We will not keep you waiting any longer than we can help."

The Judge, with an ostentatious indifference, had strolled away to the smoking-room, probably to avoid being called upon to decide so nice a point as this disputed precedence; his daughter, Miss Davenport, and Sophia had turned their backs, and, stopping their ears, were begging to be told when all was over.

Alfred was struggling to free his pistol-arm, which was firmly held by the other two men, and all three were talking at once in hot and argumentative support of their claims. As for Peter, he sat and looked on, glued to his seat by terror: if he had any preference among the disputants, he rather hoped that Alfred would be the person to gain his point.

All at once he saw Sophia turn round and, with her fingers still pressed to her ears, make energetic contortions of her lips, evidently for his benefit. After one or two repetitions, he made out the words she was voicelessly framing.

"Run for it!" he interpreted. "Quick … while you can!"

With his habitual respect for her advice, he rose and, finding that the power of motion had suddenly returned, he did run for it; he slipped quietly round the corner and down the passage to the other side of the ship, where he hoped to reach the saloon-entrance, and eventually regain his cabin.

Unhappily for him, the grim lady from Melbourne had noted his flight and anticipated its object. Long before he got to the open doors, he saw her step out and bar the way; she had an open sunshade in her hand, which she was preparing to use as a butterfly net.

He turned and fled abruptly in the opposite direction, intending to cross the bridge which led aft to the second-class saloon deck, where he might find cover: but as he saw, on turning the corner, the Manager had already occupied the passage, Peter turned again and doubled back across the ship, making for the forecastle; but he was too late, for the Melbourne man was there before him, and cut off all hope of retreat in that quarter.

There was only one thing left now: he must take to the rigging, and accordingly the next moment, scarcely knowing how he came there, he was clambering up the shrouds for dear life!

Higher and higher he climbed, slipping and stumbling, and catching his unaccustomed feet in the ratlins at every step; and all the way he had a dismal conviction that as yet he had not nearly exhausted the cheque he had drawn. He must have at least another couple of hours to get through, not to mention the compound interest, which the Bank seemed characteristically enough to be paying first.

Still, if he could only stay quietly up aloft till his time was up, he might escape the worst yet. Surely it was a sufficient penalty for his folly to have embroiled himself with every creature he knew; to have been chivied about the deck of an ocean steamer by three violent men, each thirsting for his blood; and to be reduced to mount the rigging like an escaped monkey!

A few more steps and he was safe at last! Just above was a huge yard, flattened on the upper surface, with a partially furled sail, behind which he could crouch unseen; his hands were almost upon it, when a bronzed and bearded face appeared above the canvas—it was one of the English crew.

"Beg your pardon, sir," said the man, civilly enough, "but I shall 'ave fur to trouble you to go down agin, please. Capt'in's strick orders, sir. Passengers ain't allowed to amuse theirselves climbing the rigging!"

"My good man!" said Peter, between his pants, "do I look as if I was amusing myself? I am pursued, I tell you. As an honest, good-hearted British seaman—which I am sure you are,—I entreat you to give me a hand up, and hide me: it—it may be life or death for me!"

The man wavered; the desperate plight Peter was in seemed to arouse his compassion, as it well might.

"I could 'ide yer, I suppose, come to that," he said slowly; "but it's too late to think o' that now. Look below, sir!"

Peter glanced down between his feet, and saw two swarthy Lascars climbing the rigging like cats. Lower still, he had a bird's-eye view of the deck, about which his enemies were posted in readiness for his arrival: the Manager exhibiting his spiked boots to Sir William, who shook his head in mild deprecation; the old lady brandishing her sunshade in angry denunciation, while her brother flourished his horsewhip; and Alfred stood covering him with his revolver, prepared to pick him off the instant he came within range!

And Peter hung there by his hands—for his feet had slipped out of the ratlins—as helpless a target as any innocent bottle in a shooting-gallery, and the Lascars were getting nearer and nearer!

He could see their bilious eyeballs, and their teeth gleaming in their dusky faces. He felt a bony hand reaching for his ankles, and then a dizziness came over him: his grip upon the coarse, tarry cordage relaxed, and, shutting his eyes, he fell—down—down—down. Would the fall never come to an end? Would he never arrive?...

CHAPTER X

Dénoûment

At last! The shock was over; and he feebly opened his eyes once more, to find that he was undoubtedly on the deck; and, yes, the Bank Manager was standing over him with a kind of triumphant grin!

"Mercy!" Peter murmured faintly. "You—you surely wouldn't kick a man when he's down!"

"My dear sir!" protested the Manager, "why should I wish to kick you in any position?"

He must be fatally injured, if even the Manager had relented!

"Is—is Alfred there?" asked Tourmalin, anxiously. "Keep him away, if you can!"

"Certainly!" said Mr. Perkins. "Who is Alfred?"

"Why, the—the man with the revolver. I thought you knew!"

"Come, come," said the Manager, "there's no man of that kind here, I assure you. Pull yourself together, sir; you're on board the Boomerang now!"

"I know," said Peter, dolefully,—"I know I am!"

He shut his eyes resignedly. He was about to receive some other portion of his time-balance. If he could only hope that no fresh complications would arise! Would he meet Miss Tyrrell or Miss Davenport next, he wondered, and how would they behave?

"Haven't you had sleep enough yet?" said the Manager. "You're not more than half-awake even now!"

"Sleep?" exclaimed Tourmalin, sitting up and rubbing his eyes. "Why, you don't mean to tell me I've been dreaming all this time!"

"I don't know about dreaming; but I can answer for your snoring. Why, you almost drowned the ship's band! I knew what would happen when you would have two helpings of curry at breakfast. Worst thing to take in the world, especially if you don't walk it off! Why, you've been the joke of the whole ship for the last half-hour. I wish you could have seen yourself, with your head hanging over the arm of your chair and your mouth wide open! I thought at last it was only kind to wake you up. Those two young ladies over there have been in fits of laughter!"

Peter picked up Buckle, which was lying face downwards on the deck. His own face was very red, possibly from stooping, as he inquired:

"Er—which two young ladies?"

"Can't tell you their names; but those two uncommonly nice-looking girls—one in white and navy-blue, and the darker one in pink. Dear me, I thought they would have died!"

Even now they seemed to have the greatest difficulty in controlling their countenances, for happening just then to look round and catch Peter's glance of confused and still somnolent suspicion, they buried their faces in their handkerchiefs once more, in agonies of suppressed mirth.

And these were the two whom his dreaming fancies had pictured as tenderly, desperately, madly devoted to him! The reality was decidedly disenchanting: they were very ordinary girls, he saw, after all.

"Well," said Mr. Perkins, "it's not far off tiffin time now; so, you see, you managed to get through your extra time after all!"

"Yes," said Peter, with a little natural embarrassment; "but I think, do you know, that, on reflection, I—I won't deposit the extra hours after all! If you will kindly take back the—the cheque-book," he added, feeling in his pockets, "and give me the form I signed, we will consider the arrangement cancelled—eh?"

"It's my belief," said the Manager, "that your head isn't quite clear yet; for, hang me if I know what you 're talking about! Deposit? cheque-book? form? What is it all about?"

Peter coloured more furiously than before.

"It was the curry," he said. "I wasn't quite sure whether—but it's really too absurd to explain. I am wide-awake now, at all events!"

He was awake now, and knew that no time-bargain of this monstrous kind had ever been actually effected, and all the wild events which seemed to have taken whole months to accomplish themselves, were the work of a single hour's indigestion! He was still a bachelor; still engaged to Sophia: he had still to make the acquaintance of Miss Tyrrell and Miss Davenport, and endure the ordeal of remaining for some weeks to come—to say nothing of the extra hours—exposed to the peril of their fascinations!

But whatever happened now, it could not be said, at least, that he had not received abundant warning of the consequences which might ensue from any yielding, however blameless or defensible, on his part.

And Peter Tourmalin resolved that henceforth Buckle should monopolise his attention.

THE EPILOGUE

There are always a few inquiring persons who, at the conclusion of any story, insist upon being told "what happened after that." And if such a question is ever justified, it is so in the case of a narrative that, as in the present instance, ends almost at the precise moment at which it began.

So it is not impossible that some readers may be sufficiently interested to wish to know the particular effect produced upon Peter Tourmalin's subsequent conduct by a vision more than usually complicated and connected.

Did he receive it, for example, as a solemnly prophetic warning, and forswear all female society while on board the Boomerang? or was he rather prompted to prove its fallibility by actual experience?

As to the motives which guided him, we are unable to speak with confidence, and they must be left to be accounted for by the reader's knowledge of human nature in general, and Peter's, so far as it has been self-revealed by his unconscious imagination in these pages, in particular.

But the author is in a position to state with certainty that, when Sophia and her mother met the ship, as they duly did at Gibraltar, nothing on Peter's part gave them the slightest ground for suspecting that he was on terms of even the most distant acquaintanceship with either Miss Tyrrell or Miss Davenport, and that the fact of his being far advanced in the third volume of Buckle's History of Civilisation seemed to guarantee that he had employed his spare time on board the vessel both wisely and well.

Nor did he get into any difficulties by circulating gossip concerning any matron from Melbourne, owing to the circumstance that there was no lady passenger who at all answered the description. She, like much else in his experiences, was purely a creation of the curry.

Lastly, it may be added that Peter is now married to his Sophia, and is far happier than even he could have expected. She tempers her intellectuality out of consideration for his mental bareness; and as yet he has never found her society in the least oppressive, nor has his errant fancy wandered back in any perfidious sense to the time he spent, when freed from her supervision, on board the Boomerang.

F. Anstey – A Concise Bibliography

Vice Versa (1882)
The Black Poodle And Other Tales (1884)
The Giant's Robe (1884)
The Tinted Venus (1885)
A Fallen Idol (1886)
Burglar Bill And Other Pieces (1888)
The Pariah (1889)
Voces Populi (1890)
Tourmalin's Time Cheques (1891)
Mr. Punch's Model Music-Hall Songs And Dramas (1892)
The Talking Horse And Other Tales (1892)
The Travelling Companions (1892)
The Man From Blankley's And Other Sketches (1893)

www.ingramcontent.com/pod-product-compliance
Lightning Source LLC
Chambersburg PA
CBHW061455170626
46811CB00004B/1523